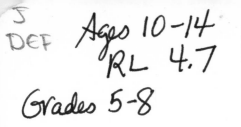

NEW MILFORD PUBLIC LIBRARY

P9-BYB-503

DATE DUE

DEC 2009

Also by Cynthia DeFelice

siGNAL

siGNAL

CYNTHIA DeFELICE

FARRAR, STRAUS AND GIROUX
NEW YORK

Copyright © 2009 by Cynthia C. DeFelice
All rights reserved
Distributed in Canada by Douglas & McIntyre Ltd.
Printed in July 2009 in the United States of America
by RR Donnelley, Harrisonburg, Virginia
Designed by Jaclyn Sinquett
First edition, 2009
1 3 5 7 9 10 8 6 4 2

www.fsgkidsbooks.com

Library of Congress Cataloging-in-Publication Data
DeFelice, Cynthia C.
    Signal / Cynthia DeFelice.— 1st ed.
        p. cm.
    Summary: After moving with his distant father to the Finger Lakes
region of New York, twelve-year-old Owen faces a lonely summer until
he meets an abused girl who may be a space alien.
    ISBN-13: 978-0-374-39915-3
    [1. Friendship—Fiction.   2. Loneliness—Fiction.   3. Child abuse—
Fiction.   4. Emotional problems—Fiction.   5. Moving, Household—
Fiction.]   I. Title.

PZ7.D3597 Si 2009
[Fic]—dc22

                                                            2008009278

To my starbabies, Annabelle and Elizabeth, with love

SIGNAL

1

If I were an animal, what kind would I be? Well, that's a really interesting question, Josie. I have a lot of favorites. Obviously, no animal is nobler than the dog."

Josie, who is running ahead of me, glances back and gives me a knowing look.

"But I think I'd be a falcon. They can dive at speeds up to two hundred miles an hour. How cool would that be? Falcons fly and hunt wherever they please. They *rule* the sky."

Josie gives a yip and takes off after a squirrel. Okay, I admit it, Josie's my dog. I'm talking to my dog. Maybe it's pathetic, but I don't have anyone else to talk to.

And Josie's terrific company, let me make that clear. I have great respect for dogs in general and Josie in particular. We got her when I was five, and she's always been my best friend. Since we moved here when school ended in June, she's my only friend.

Here is upstate New York, in what everybody calls the Finger Lakes region. That's because there are eleven long, narrow lakes that look like skinny fingers. Most of them have Iroquois Indian names, like Seneca, Canandaigua, Keuka, and Cayuga. I can't remember them all.

The lakes were made by glaciers during the Ice Age, but there's an Iroquois legend that says they were formed when the Great Spirit reached down and pressed his hands into the earth. Which is kind of cool to think about, except I can't help wondering if there's another legend that explains why the Great Spirit had eleven fingers.

I like to picture those giant hands reaching down from the sky. In my mind, they're always hairy, with five fingers on one hand and six on the other.

Anyway, I'm not saying I was Mr. Popularity at my old school, but I had buddies. I miss Kevin Bowen the most. He and I did practically everything together. We were known as "Owen and Bowen." I'm Owen, obviously. Owen McGuire.

Take it from me, you don't want to move at the end of the school year. Because then there you are in a new place where you don't know anybody, and you've got the whole summer ahead of you.

We only moved a few hours away, but it feels really different here. In Buffalo, our house was in a neighborhood with a lot of kids. But now we live in what you'd have to call the boonies. There's Seneca Lake to the east, the highway to the west, and everywhere else, nothing but woods and farm fields. I like living in the country and seeing all the deer and turkeys and woodchucks, but it would be nice to see some people, too. Especially another twelve-year-old kid.

When we first got here at the end of June, I rode around on my bike to check things out. That's when I discovered the trail I'm running on now. It's seven miles long, and follows the path of a stream that runs between our lake, Seneca, and Keuka Lake. The stream has cut steep cliffs through the woods, and it's cool and shady down there. That makes it a perfect place for running, which I'm doing every day. The school I'll be going to in the fall has a soccer team for grades seven and eight, and I plan to be on it. I decided I might as well use this long summer on my own to get in shape and practice my footwork.

So Josie and I have been running every day for three and a half weeks, going about three miles up the trail and three miles back, sometimes even more. We've seen a lot of amazing stuff. Like one day Josie came toward me howling like a crazy thing, chasing a wild turkey. It flew down the trail right at me, madly flapping its wings, and just missed the top of my head. I could feel the rush of air from its wings in my hair.

Another day a black bear was standing in the trail ahead of us. Josie and I both stopped dead in our tracks.

We looked at the bear, and the bear looked at us. I glanced down at Josie, and every hair on her body was standing out so stiffly she looked a lot bigger than her normal size.

"Easy, girl," I murmured. She gave a funny little growl, and the bear ambled away. It didn't seem to want anything to do with us, but we headed back the way we had come, just in case.

Then, two days ago, Josie ran ahead and started barking at something on the path. I nearly had a heart attack when I saw it was a snapping turtle as big as home plate. Josie was dancing all around it, lunging in and out, yipping with excitement.

"No, Josie!" I cried, but she didn't stop. "Josie! If that thing clamps its jaws onto your nose, you are going to be very sorry!" I warned.

Finally, I was able to grab her collar and drag her away, but I could tell she wanted to go back there in the worst way. There are some things she's not real smart about.

I don't know the names of every single tree and plant and bird and animal we've been seeing on our runs, but I know a lot of them. When I was little, my mom gave me a set of field guides. She and Josie and I used to take long walks, and when we got home, we'd look up everything we'd seen in the books. I have guides on birds, mammals, reptiles and amphibians, wildflowers, rocks and fossils, insects, and stars. The one on stars and planets is my favorite. It was Mom's, too.

It was Mom who really taught me to notice things. So I keep my eyes open on my runs with Josie. I recognize the teeny heart-shaped tracks of fawns and the handlike prints of raccoons. By now I know the squawk of the great blue heron that we scare out of its favorite minnow-hunting spot, and the musky smell foxes leave behind. I like to look for trout and suckers in the pools of the stream, and Josie keys me in to every squirrel, rabbit, and woodchuck we pass by.

When you're running along through all that nature, it's easy to see how everything belongs. Every animal and plant has its place in the big picture. So things that *don't* belong really stand out, like a soda bottle, or candy bar wrapper, or a deflated Mylar party balloon. It ticks me off that people throw stuff like that around, and I've made it my mission to pick up trash I see and carry it out if I can.

Up ahead, I see something white lying off the path near a patch of raspberry bushes. Josie goes over to it, sniffs, then picks it up and runs along with it in her mouth.

"Josie, come!" I shout. She's always finding stinky dead animals and scraps of food people have left behind, stuff she thinks is wonderful. This looks like a paper towel or a napkin, maybe. At least it doesn't look like anything too disgusting, not that that would have stopped Josie.

She comes and I say, "Sit, Josie. Drop it." Josie is a German shorthaired pointer, a hunting dog, so she's supposed to surrender whatever she retrieves to me, her owner, the mighty hunter.

Amazingly, she sits at my first command and drops what I see now is a piece of white cloth.

"Good dog!"

There's red stuff on it. I start to pick it up, wondering what the red is. Paint?

Whoa. Gross. Quickly, I throw it back to the ground. The red stuff is, I'm pretty sure, blood. The cloth is soft and stretchy, and has a ragged edge. It looks like it was torn off the bottom of somebody's T-shirt.

Yuck. I'm not carrying *that* out, never mind my good intentions about trash removal.

I start running again. Being on the trail makes me think of all the outdoor things Mom and I used to do together. I remember a clear winter night when I was eight years old. Dad was working late. Mom got me all bundled up in my snowsuit and hat and mittens and boots, and we went outside and lay down on our backs in the snow and stared up at the sky. I barely even felt the cold because I was really noticing for the first time how enormous the sky is.

Mom told me how far away the stars are and I couldn't believe it. I asked, "Where does it *end*?" Mom said she didn't know. I kept trying to picture where the universe stopped, but I couldn't do it. You can't picture *nothing*, because as soon as you do, it's *something*.

Then Mom said, "There are eight hundred thousand galaxies and billions of stars and planets out there. I like to imagine that one of them is the sun in a solar system similar to ours."

I liked imagining it, too.

When we finally got cold and went inside, we read in the field guide to stars and planets that the number of stars is so huge that "the statistical possibility of other solar systems definitely exists." I memorized that sentence. The book also said that telescopes have shown that there are millions of galaxies beyond ours.

Mom said, "Nobody knows exactly what happened to create the Earth's solar system, Owen. But I don't see any reason to think it happened only once. It's such a small view of things, don't you agree?"

I did. I certainly didn't want to be the kind of person who had a small view of things. To me, it was logical to think there would be life beyond our one little planet. Actually, it seemed crazy to think there *wouldn't* be.

After that night, I read everything I could about space, spaceships, space travel, people's accounts of their encounters with aliens, you name it. I became convinced that not only is there life on other planets, but that they've been trying to contact us. Mom thought so, too.

Thinking about Mom is making me miss her, so I take a pretend head shot and resume my conversation with Josie. "Yes, Josie, you're right. I learned all my cool soccer moves from Dad. You know the goal we have set up in the yard where we practice taking shots after dinner? I'm getting pretty good, don't you think? I can't wait for our trip to Alaska in August. Yeah, you can come, too. Didn't we take you along when we camped in the Rockies and went fishing in the Everglades?"

Josie sniffs when I say this. She knows it's all a lie. Dad and I never go on cool trips together. There's no soccer goal in our yard. I'm just learning to play, and Dad doesn't. Play, I mean. Not soccer, not anything. Today is Sunday, and where is Dad? At work. He's always been the World's Most Dedicated Accountant, but it seems to me he started working even more after Mom died.

It was a car accident. A snowy January night a year and a half ago. She skidded into a tree on her way back from work. I was home when it happened, watching the storm out the window, urging the snow to come down faster and heavier so school would be canceled.

I don't even remember if it was or not.

For Dad and me, a huge, jagged hole suddenly opened up in our lives. We just tiptoed around it, as if maybe it would go away if we pretended hard enough.

It didn't go away. It just got bigger and deeper.

Dad and I don't talk about it. It's just the way it is.

I don't want to think about all that, and besides, Josie has gone racing ahead—too far ahead. She's really fast. For every mile I go, I bet she does five or six. She needs the exercise. As long as she gets a nice, long run every day, she's what I'm sure anyone would agree is the perfect dog. She's good even if she has to be cooped up for a couple days, but it's hard for her.

I can relate. After all, I've told her, I have to go to school.

I whistle and she comes back—with another scrap of the same T-shirt-like material in her mouth. It has a smear of bright red blood on it. When blood is still red instead of brown, it's, like, *fresh*, right?

I look around uneasily, but there's nobody else in sight. This is starting to freak me out. Let's face it; blood is creepy stuff.

Josie has taken off again, and I shrug and follow her. I wonder if it's a person or an animal that's bleeding and then realize it's a stupid question: animals don't rip up their T-shirts to blot their cuts. Probably somebody sneezed and got a bloody nose, or got scratched while picking raspberries. But what if it's something worse? I wonder if I should get help.

When we moved and it looked like I was going to be on my own for most of the summer, Dad gave me a cell phone. I could call him now. Or 911. But is this an emergency? I'm not sure. I take the phone from my pocket and turn it on. No reception. It must be because of the high cliffs on both sides of the stream.

I put the phone away and scan the ground. The trail is soft and moist here and I see footprints. Feeling like a real tracker, I stop to study them. They have the pattern of sneakers or running shoes, like the ones I'm wearing, but since they're only partial prints I can't get a sense of the size. Josie comes over and examines them, too, but doesn't seem to find them very interesting. They're not animal tracks, after all.

Then I notice that the person who made the prints has left the trail. There is an old, dilapidated mill ahead on the left. On the right is a meadow of tall grass, and it's clear someone has recently moved through it. I follow the path of broken, mashed-down stalks of grass, wondering what in the world I'm doing, but doing it anyway.

Josie apparently thinks this detour from the trail is great fun, because she bounds ahead of me, making her own path through the undergrowth. The meadow ends at a steep shale slope, and I can see an avalanche of thin, crumbly stones that were sent cascading down it by the person ahead of me, who I'm beginning to think of as "the bloody guy."

So I climb the slope, too, annoyed by the ease with which Josie manages the slippery shale incline that has me on all fours, panting and clutching at anything that looks solid. It's like climbing a sand dune, so with each step I slide back half a step.

When I get to the top of the hill, I see a house that seems to be abandoned. There are no cars, and the grass is overgrown. Beyond the house is a cornfield, a monster cornfield, and alongside that is an equally huge wheat field. Both of them stretch as far as I can see into the distance.

The guy's track leads right to the edge of the corn.

It's late July and we've had a lot of rain, and the cornstalks are already higher than the top of my head. They are planted right up to the edge of the yard, crowding the house, standing in silent rows and shimmering in the hushed, hot, humid air. I stand at the edge of the field where the bloody guy went in, wondering if I should bother to follow him.

I take a few steps into the corn, and that's all it takes to feel as if I've been transported to an entirely different world. The plants are so high and so thick that things look the same in every direction. I feel *swallowed up* by the corn. I fight back a panicky claustrophobia and realize that I'd never be able to find the bloody guy in here if he didn't want me to—and it's pretty obvious he *doesn't* want me to, since he seems to be purposely hiding from me.

I want to get out of that cornfield as fast as I can. I'm about to turn and retrace my steps when I hear a sound coming from out of the greenness growing all around me. I cock my head and listen closely. There it is again. Breathing. Hard breathing.

The bloody guy *is* in the corn, and not far away. He has to know I'm here, and yet he isn't saying hello or asking for help. He's hiding. And panting.

A breeze stirs the corn. The tops sigh gently, and the lower, more dried-out leaves make a clacking sound against each other. Suddenly I'm more spooked than I've ever been in my life. I turn and run out into the open air and across the farmyard. "Josie! Come!" I call. I slip and slide down that shale cliff, land at the bottom in a tangle of limbs and loose rock, then get up and run, run, run back down the trail, wanting nothing but to put distance between me and whoever is breathing out there in the corn.

2

I SPEND THE AFTERNOON THROWING A BALL FOR Josie and thinking about the bloody guy. Then, just when I'm expecting Dad to come home for dinner, he calls to tell me he's tied up at work and won't be home until close to nine o'clock.

"Dad, it's *Sunday*," I say.

He sighs. "I know, Owen. But this is my first big audit, and the client is very important to the firm."

I look around at the living room, where cardboard boxes still line the walls, right where the moving guys left them. "I thought we were going to unpack some of this stuff today. You know, get moved in."

Another sigh. "I hoped we could, buddy, but there's no way it's going to happen today. Listen, there's some leftover fried chicken and cole slaw in the fridge, right?"

"I don't know. I guess so."

"You can warm the chicken up in the microwave."

"Okay."

"Sorry, Owen. I'll get home just as soon as I can. Call if you need anything."

"Okay, Dad. See you."

I feed Josie, nuke the chicken, and sit down in front of the TV. I barely even notice what's on, because I keep thinking about the bloody guy who was hiding in the cornfield. I try to imagine what happened to him and why he didn't want me to see him. It's odd. It's mysterious. It's fun to have something new to think about.

∘—∘—∘

The next morning, Dad has already left for work by the time I get up and have a quick breakfast. Josie picks up one of my running shoes, drops it at my feet, and wags her tail expectantly. I get on my bike and head for the trail. Josie trots along by my front wheel, on the side away from the traffic on the highway. I never taught her this; she just figured it out on her own.

I park my bike at the trailhead and lock it, and Josie and I start our run. We're heading back to the place where I heard the bloody guy breathing. I'm curious, excited—and scared.

I look around with more attention than usual, but there's nothing out of the ordinary on the trail this morning. The sun is shining through the mist that's rising off the bushes and trees, and it's so peaceful and pretty that the panic and fear I felt yesterday seem ridiculous.

But when I get to the meadow near the shale slope, my feet start to falter. Some of that fear and panic sets back in. I'm also feeling kind of ashamed that I ran away. Maybe the guy actually *did* need help, but was afraid of *me* for some reason.

The path through the meadow is faintly visible, although most of the grass has perked up. I follow it to the bottom of the hill, and climb.

At the top, I stand for a while looking around and catching my breath. The cornfield is as huge as I remember, stretching endlessly in a sea of sameness that could hide an army. No sense looking there.

I check out the house, which is clearly deserted but doesn't seem as if it's been left for too long. It doesn't have that haunted house look that places get when they've been neglected for years, with drooping shutters, peeling paint, broken windows, and the smell of rot and decay. This place looks unlived in, but like you *could* live in it if you wanted to and you felt like doing some fixing up. Josie is sniffing around the foundation, probably hunting for mice.

I walk closer, and then climb three wooden steps up to the porch. My hand reaches out to try the doorknob. If it's locked, I'll leave; there's no way I'm going to break in.

The knob turns, and I see the lock is broken. I push the door open and step into the kitchen. It smells hot and musty inside, but not bad. There's a table with four chairs around it, and a refrigerator, stove, and sink. Exactly what you'd expect to see. I turn the cold water handle, and nothing comes out. The counters are bare but dusty. There's a cupboard door hanging open and I can see the shelves inside are empty.

I walk across the floor. Josie follows me, her toenails clicking on the cracked linoleum. We go through an arched opening that leads to what I figure is the living room. There's a couch with some of the stuffing coming out of the cushions, a fireplace, and a rickety table that looks like it would collapse if you put anything heavier than a napkin on it.

The house feels so still and empty I have the odd sensation that it's holding its breath until I leave. But I'm not ready to go quite yet. I peek into a room that looks like it was an office, and into a bathroom. In the office I see a couple of broken pencil stubs and some scraps of paper; in the bathroom, a box of tissues and a spray bottle of cleaning stuff lying on its side. Nothing very exciting, and I feel my interest waning.

But there is a stairway to a second floor, and it seems dumb to leave without going up there and checking it out, although going *upstairs* in a stranger's house seems like more of an invasion of privacy than poking around downstairs. Or at least that's what I think as I climb the first couple steps. Josie stays at the bottom, whining at me beseechingly, but when I keep going she decides to come along and races past me.

There are two rooms and another bathroom on the second floor. The first room has flowered wallpaper and holds a metal bed frame with a grungy-looking mattress on it, and a dresser, its empty drawers open. The bathroom has an old-fashioned-looking tub with a plastic shower curtain, and some sort of frilly, lacy thing over the toilet tank. That cracks me up. As if nobody's going to notice there's a toilet under it.

Josie runs ahead of me and starts to bark. I hear the dancing sound her paws make when she wiggles her whole body in delight at seeing a new person. Then I hear a muffled scream and I feel like my stomach just jumped up into my throat. I stop walking. Part of me wants to blow out of there as fast as possible, but another part draws me forward and into the other bedroom. The bloody guy is sitting up, looking at me.

Except the bloody guy is a girl.

3

SHE'S A GIRL ABOUT MY AGE, I REALIZE AFTER I recover from my shock and surprise. She's sitting up on the mattress, clutching what's left of a torn white T-shirt around her. She has the oddest, greenest, most glittery eyes I've ever seen, and they glare at me with a mixture of fear and defiance. She's wearing dirty shorts. A makeshift bandage tied around her head has slipped out of place and now hangs crookedly over her right eye. There's a bad cut there, and more cuts on her arms and legs, which are streaked with dirt and dried blood. Her light brown hair is tangled and caked with blood above the cut.

Her lips look pale and cracked and dry. My own mouth and throat feel dry just looking at her.

Maybe she feels as stunned as I do, because we both stay right where we are, staring, like we're playing some weird game of freeze tag. Finally, Josie breaks the spell, looking back and forth from the girl to me and barking as if she's urging us to *get on with it*, whatever it is we're doing.

I have no idea what we're doing, or what *she's* doing, anyway, sleeping all by herself in a deserted house with cuts on her head, arms, and legs. At last I manage to ask, "What happened to you?"

She keeps looking at me but doesn't reply, almost as if that question is too big to even start answering. Or maybe her throat is too dry. So I say the next thing that comes to my mind. "You want some water?"

There's a long drawn-out silence, and I'm starting to wonder if the injury to her head has made her stupid, or if she's deaf or mute or something, or if maybe she doesn't understand English. But then she nods, just slightly.

"Okay, I'll go get some." I head—fast—straight to the stairs and down and out the door, Josie at my heels.

My mind is racing, thinking about water. I could go to the creek by the trail to get some, but I don't have a container to put it in and besides, even though people swim in the creek, including me, I'm not sure the water is safe to actually drink. Of course, Josie drinks it every day. This doesn't prove anything, though, because in general the more unsanitary something is the better Josie likes it.

I decide the only thing to do is go back to the trail-head where I left my bike. I keep a bottle of water in the clip on the handlebar stem for slugging down at the end of my run. As I race along the path, I wonder about the girl. I wonder why I didn't ask her more questions, and I guess it was because there was something so odd and unsettling about her and her glittery eyes and her blood-streaked appearance.

When I reach my bike I get on and head back up the trail. I don't try to ride through the meadow, but stay on the trail until I get close to the hill that leads up to the farmhouse. By then, Josie is panting from running beside me, so I let her take a long drink from the stream. Then I stash the bike in some bushes near the hill and begin to climb. It's harder with one hand holding the bottle, and I finally stick it in the waistband of my shorts.

When I get to the top and look at the house, I have the feeling that the girl won't be there when I go in. But she's waiting in the kitchen. I catch a glimpse of her peering from behind the door before she opens it. I hand her the water bottle and I watch her throat as she throws back her head and gulps greedily until it's empty.

After that, it's like neither one of us knows what to do. Her eyes flicker past me toward the door, which I've left open. She licks her dry lips. She says, "You came back," and her voice is all croaky and hoarse.

There doesn't seem to be anything to say to that. I mean, here I am.

She clears her throat and says, "You're not going to tell, are you." It's a statement, not a question.

Tell *who what*? I wonder. But I shake my head no.

This seems to satisfy her, because she nods and says, "And you'll help me."

"I *got* water," I point out, in case she hadn't noticed I'd already helped.

"With everything," she says patiently.

Again, it doesn't really sound like a question. And, even though I don't know what I'm agreeing to, I nod.

"This is an excellent place," she says.

Well, yeah, I think, *for a deserted house.* "What do you mean? You're not going to stay here, are you?"

"Temporarily."

"How long?"

"Until they come for me." She looks at Josie, who is sniffing around aimlessly, and smiles. "They like dogs."

Now I'm really starting to wonder if getting conked on the head messed up her mind. Who's coming? And so what if they like dogs?

Then she says, "I'm Campion."

I stare at her, wondering yet again what in the world she's talking about. "Camping?" I repeat. "Okay. I guess this is kind of like camping out, except you're camping *in.*"

She doesn't even smile at my dumb joke. "Campion. It's my name."

"Oh," I say, feeling foolish. "First or last?"

"First," she says and looks at me expectantly. I realize this would be the time for me to identify myself, too. "Owen McGuire," I say, adding, "I never heard of anybody named Campion before."

"I was named for a wildflower," she says. "But there are flowers with worse names. I could have been called Humped Bladderwort or Hairy Vetch."

I laugh, surprised, and she gives me a funny little smile in return. Her whole face changes when she smiles, and she doesn't look quite so strange and fierce.

"Red campion is an alien species," she says, in a voice like she's reading from a book, "alien meaning 'from someplace else, but managing to survive here.' " She looks at me with her eyebrows raised, as if this is important information, but I don't get what the big deal is.

"Campion thrives on roadsides and in waste places," she says. Then she gives me that odd, quick smile again. "Which pretty much says it all. Anyway, you can call me Cam."

"Okay," I say.

"I need you to bring me food and drinks," she says. "I'm not a picky eater. Anything is fine. A towel. Soap, a toothbrush, and toothpaste. A comb. Or a brush—doesn't matter. A couple of T-shirts. Do you have any shorts or pants that would fit me? Or, if not, maybe a belt or some rope or something in case they're too big?"

"I guess," I say. I'm feeling a little bit annoyed. I mean, sure, I want to help her, and I can see she needs some different clothes. But she's pretty bossy, if you ask me. Does she expect me to be her delivery boy? What's next, I wonder, hot pizza?

"It got cold last night," she says. "Could you bring a blanket and maybe a sweatshirt?"

"Sure," I say, "but hold on just a second. How about first-aid stuff? Actually, shouldn't you go to the hospital?"

"Absolutely not," she says firmly. "No hospitals."

"I know you can't see yourself, but you look"—I hesitate, because it seems kind of rude, but then I say it anyway—"*awful.*"

"Oh, I'm sure it looks worse than it is," she says breezily. "These are just scratches on my arms and legs."

They look like a lot more than scratches to me. Before I can say anything, she goes on. "And head wounds always bleed a lot. It has something to do with all the blood vessels or veins or something."

She sounds pretty sure of herself. I have so many questions, I hardly know where to begin. "You said somebody's coming. Who?"

"My parents," she says calmly. "But not for a few days."

"Why a few days?"

"I've got to let them know where I am."

"So come to my house and call them. Or—here." I reach into my pocket for the phone. "You can use this." Then I remember it didn't work on the trail. When I turn it on, I see there's no service here, either.

She shakes her head patiently. "It doesn't work that way."

I'm really confused now. "Why not? Where are they?"

She looks up at me from under the makeshift bandage tied around her head, and those green eyes of hers bore into mine. "At home," she says.

"Where's that?" I ask, trying not to sound as impatient as I feel.

"Up there," she says, pointing to the sky. "On my home planet." Her face glows and her green eyes glitter. "You can't even imagine how wonderful it is there."

4

FOR A MINUTE WE JUST STARE AT EACH OTHER. MY mind is racing. After all my daydreaming about meeting an alien, can it actually be happening?

I stare at Cam. She doesn't look very . . . *alien.* Whatever that means. Except for those amazing green eyes.

She's got to be kidding, right?

The silence starts to grow uncomfortable, and I give a shaky laugh and say, "You mean—? Wait. Really? You're saying you're actually from another planet?"

"Yeah," she says matter-of-factly. "We were here on an exploratory mission. I was supposed to stay in the ship—"

I interrupt. "You're talking about a *spaceship*? What did it look like?"

She sighs impatiently. "Like a *spaceship.*"

"A flying saucer?" I persist.

"Technology on my planet is so advanced, it's hard to explain," she says.

"Oh," I say, disappointed. I want to tell her to at least *try* to explain it, but she keeps talking.

"I was supposed to stay in the ship, but I was curious, so I got out to see what was going on. Then jeeps full of soldiers with guns drove up, and the ship had to make a really fast emergency exit. I got left behind. So now I need to signal my parents so they can find me when they come back."

I take a seat in one of the chairs at the kitchen table to think about this. I can picture it all happening. But I have a question. "If the soldiers saw the spaceship, how come it wasn't all over the news?"

She shrugs.

I think about it, then answer my own question. "I bet the government covered it up!" I exclaim. "Like they did in Roswell, New Mexico."

Cam looks puzzled.

"You probably know all about that," I say.

She shakes her head.

"A spaceship crashed in New Mexico in 1947, and the military covered it up. They said it was just a weather balloon. But lots of people—including me, by the way—don't believe that for a second. There were witnesses who—"

Cam sits down suddenly, saying, "I feel dizzy. I'm really hungry."

"Oh!" I say. "Yeah, you must be. When did you eat last, anyway?"

She thinks for a moment. "Saturday morning."

"Wow." I'm amazed. "That's two days ago! I can't imagine going one day without eating." I think about it and amend my position. "Not even half a day. So, okay, you need food right away. I'll go get some. But when I come back, will you tell me—"

"Whatever you want to know," she says.

I get up and head to the door. I'm about to leave when she says softly, "It's no accident that you're the one who found me."

"Huh?" I say. "What do you mean?"

Those green eyes look into mine. "Lots of people wouldn't believe me," she says.

I don't know what to say. I *want* to believe her. It's certainly possible. I mean, why would she make up something like that? And I have to admit there's something about her that's different from other girls I know, and it's not just her eyes.

I mumble that I'd better get going, and Josie and I head for the trail. I pedal at a medium speed so Josie can keep up, my mind going round and round about my incredible conversation with Cam.

My thoughts are interrupted by the arrival of two familiar vans, pulling into one of the trailhead parking areas. They belong to a man and woman I call the Dog People. They seem to come here almost as often as Josie and I do. They park, open the doors, and let out a pack of dogs of all shapes and sizes. I'm not talking about two or three dogs, I mean a *pack*. Who has that many dogs?

The lady has streaky gray, tangled hair sticking out from under a battered brown hat. She's dressed, as usual, in a baggy shirt, jeans, and knee-high rubber boots. The man has shaggy hair, too, and a full beard, and when he smiles, which he does now, you can see his gnarly-looking teeth.

You'd think they'd be sick of dogs, but the man and woman both call a big hello to Josie. They know her name because it's sewn right into her collar. They always have Milk-Bones in their pockets, and Josie knows it. She runs right up to the woman and sits. The woman laughs and gives her a treat.

I smile and call, "Thanks!" But I keep on pedaling, because I know from experience how wild their dogs are when they hit the trail. Sure enough, the pack is racing everywhere, barking and wrestling with one another and with Josie. The noise is deafening. Some of them follow Josie and me for a while, completely ignoring the Dog People, who are both calling, "Popeye! Lulu! Jasper! Simone! Come!"

Finally, the dogs give up and go back, and I ride along, wondering as I always do why anybody would want to own so many dogs. That reminds me of Campion's strange comment that her alien parents "like dogs," and I smile. She should meet these people!

At home, I raid the kitchen, bathroom, and my

closet. Everything fits into the big backpack Dad gave me last Christmas, along with a tent and sleeping bag, for a camping trip that never happened.

Then I remember something Cam said to me just before I left her.

"Do you think you could get some Tootsie Rolls?"

"Tootsie Rolls?" I'd repeated.

She'd smiled and said that, as far as she was concerned, Tootsie Rolls were the single best thing about Earth.

So I take some of my allowance money, too, and before Josie and I begin our third trip down the trail, we stop at the gas station and convenience store on the corner near the trailhead. I take off the pack and set it on the ground by my bike.

Josie comes inside with me, even though there's a law that says dogs can't go into food stores. Mr. Powers, the old guy who owns the store, doesn't care about rules like that. I've gotten to know him a little bit. He sits in the store listening to his police scanner all day, and seems glad to see Josie and me when we stop in to get snacks and drinks.

Josie runs right up to the counter and sits, looking at him expectantly, since he always gives her a Slim Jim. Today Mr. Powers is talking to another customer, so I hang back, and Josie waits politely.

Over the blare of the police scanner, I hear the customer say, ". . . seen a kid? A girl, kinda skinny, light brown hair, green eyes?"

I jerk to attention when I hear this. Who else could he be talking about but Cam?

Mr. Powers seems to be considering the question, and after a few seconds the guy adds impatiently, "Might have had a cut on her head. Could have been acting funny, saying crazy things."

Slowly, Mr. Powers looks the man up and down before answering. I check him out, too. From behind, where I'm standing, I can see he's strong and solid. He's wearing black jeans, black boots, and a shirt with the sleeves cut off. It stretches tightly over the bunchy-looking muscles of his back. His neck is so thick it comes straight down from his shaved, sunburned head. A key ring hanging from his belt catches my eye. Dangling from it, along with a bunch of keys, is a shiny metal skull with red jeweled eyes.

Who is this guy and why is he looking for Cam? He's so creepy I don't even consider telling him anything.

"Can't say as I've seen anybody like that," Mr. Powers answers at last.

The man lets out a disgusted sigh and mutters a swear word under his breath. He turns to go and practically bumps into me. I back away, saying, "Sorry," and our eyes lock for a second. He swats his arm in my direction, not hitting me, but as if I'm a pesky bug he's shooing out of his way.

After he pushes through the door, I watch him out the window. He takes the keys from his belt and gets into a car, where a woman is waiting. All I can see of her is her blond hair. The car is maroon and white, rusty, and patched with dull gray body filler. The black skin on the convertible top has ragged holes in it. The car looks spotty and diseased. When it takes off, a cloud of dust and exhaust hangs over the gravel parking lot.

I go up to the counter, where Mr. Powers is feeding Josie a Slim Jim.

"You're a good old hound dog," he says to her. The first day we came to the store Mr. Powers declared Josie a hound dog, and I've stopped trying to explain that she's a pointer, not a hound. When I tried, he shook his finger in my face, lifted one of the long white eyebrows that look like two fuzzy caterpillars crawling over his saggy eyes, and said, "I raised bluetick hounds as a young man, sonny, and I know a hound dog when I see one. This here is a hound dog."

I figure if he wants to think Josie is a hound dog it's okay with me. He's always nice to her, and to me, too, even if he is a little strange.

Mr. Powers turns the scanner down a bit. "You know that fella?" he asks as he reaches into the jar of jaw-breakers, selects one, and rolls it across the counter to me.

I shrug. "No."

"You seen the girl he was asking about?"

"No," I say quickly, startled that he'd asked me.

Mr. Powers's blue eyes penetrate mine. "Sure about that?" he asks.

"Yeah, I'm sure," I say, trying to sound firm. Then, "Why?"

"You're acting kinda jumpy, is all."

"I'm not jumpy," I say, trying to sound offhand and nonchalant. I know I'm not a very smooth liar, and Mr. Powers is making me nervous.

"Hmmph," he says, which could mean he believes me, or not. I'm afraid he's going to continue with this line of questioning, but instead he says, "So, what can I do for you today?"

I'm so rattled from the guy asking about Cam and from Mr. Powers's questions to me that for a second I can't think why I'm here. Then I remember. I take a bag of miniature Tootsie Rolls from the shelf and put it on the counter. I pay quickly and leave. As I bike up the trail, I decide to give Cam a chance to eat before I tell her about the scary guy who is looking for her.

5

WHEN JOSIE AND I GET TO THE HOUSE, CAM IS waiting in the kitchen. I announce each item as I take it from the pack and set it on the table: "Shorts, belt, T-shirt, sweatshirt, blanket, soap, towel, toothbrush, toothpaste, comb, more water, and—whether you want them or not—bandages and first-aid cream."

Cam smiles but continues to eye the pack hungrily. I grin. On purpose, I've saved the food for last. I call out: "Mountain Dew, Oreos, chips, crackers and cheese, bananas, an apple, granola bars, and four cans of tuna. I even remembered a fork. *And* ta-da!" With a dramatic flourish, I take out the Tootsie Rolls and hold them up.

Cam gasps, grabs the bag from my hand, rips it open, unwraps a Tootsie Roll, and stuffs it into her mouth. As she eats it, she unwraps another one.

I laugh and say, "So, on your planet people eat dessert before dinner?"

She gives me a gooey brown smile and says, "You betcha. I just love these things. When I go back home, I'm taking as many as I can with me."

I laugh again.

She offers me the bag. It's hard to talk when you have a mouth full of Tootsie Roll, so it's quiet for a while except for the sounds of our chewing. Then Cam turns to the food on the table.

Spread out like that, it doesn't exactly make up what Mr. Lauer, my old health teacher, would call a balanced meal. But fruit's good, right? And tuna has protein. I didn't think to bring mayonnaise or bread so she could make a sandwich, and I say so.

"Tuna's better straight out of the can, anyway," she says. She pulls the tab on one of the tins, digs the fork in, and eats ravenously, not looking up until it's gone.

"Here you go, Josie," she says, putting the empty tin on the floor. Quickly, Cam eats the rest of the tuna. We watch Josie, laughing as she pushes the cans across the floor and into the corner, where she licks them like crazy to get every last molecule of flavor out.

Cam washes down a granola bar with a can of soda, then settles into a kitchen chair with the apple and a contented sigh.

I figure the time has come. "Cam," I say, "we've got to talk."

"Okay. What about?"

"If I'm going to help you, you've got to tell me what's going on."

She nods again.

"For starters, if you're from another planet, how come there was a guy asking about you at the corner store?"

Cam's head snaps up, and her green eyes flash with alarm. "Who was he?" she asks.

"You tell me."

"What did he look like?"

"Like a bald-headed pit bull with a big, fat neck."

She rises to her feet, her face paling beneath its tan. "Did you see what kind of car he was driving?"

"Rusty old junker, all patched together with Bondo. Oh, and he had a key ring with a skull and—"

"Red eyes." She covers her face with her hands and says, "*Ray.*"

In this single word I hear dismay, hatred, and fear.

She uncovers her face. "Was he alone?"

"There was a lady out in the car."

"Blond hair?"

I nod.

"Could they have followed you?"

"No," I quickly assure her. "I don't think the lady saw me, and anyway, they left before I did. The guy was asking Mr. Powers, the old man who owns the store, if he'd seen a kid—and, well, he described you." I hesitate, then add, "He said your head might have been hurt, and that you could be acting funny, saying crazy things."

As I say this I'm thinking, *Like saying you're from another planet.*

Cam snorts and says bitterly, "Yeah, he's afraid I'll say crazy things like he hit me."

Abruptly, she looks away from me, and I see that she is struggling not to cry.

"Cam," I say. "This guy Ray, who is he?"

Cam sinks back into her chair. "You really want to hear all this?"

"Well. Yeah. I feel totally clueless here."

She waits a few moments before saying, "You remember how I told you my parents' spaceship had to make an emergency exit, right?"

I nod.

"They didn't know I wasn't on the ship and after I saw them leave, I ran from the soldiers and hid. I waited for a long time, hoping my parents would come back for me, even though I knew it was too risky for them with all the attention we'd attracted. I was scared, and I didn't know what else to do. Finally, I got really hungry and thirsty, so I started walking. I came to a place with lots of houses and hid behind one of them. That's where Bobbi found me. She's the blond woman in the car."

"Did you tell her you were left behind by a spaceship?"

"No," Cam says. "For all I knew, she would have handed me over to the soldiers. So I told her I'd run away from home.

"She didn't ask any questions. She just said, 'Yeah, I know what that's like.' Then she said I could stay with her until I figured things out. I don't know why. I was just thankful."

Cam pauses, and I'm so involved in her story that I just wait, silently urging her to go on.

"So I stayed there, trying not to do anything to make Bobbi change her mind and kick me out. I just needed a place to stay until I could signal my parents. Bobbi wasn't around much. She was a bartender down the street at a place called the Blue Eagle.

"The first week everything was okay. But then Bobbi met up with Ray. She said she used to date him before and they were getting back together. Don't ask me why she likes him. He's mean when he's drinking, which is pretty much all the time. She even let him move in with us—just like that—and things got bad real fast. There were a lot of fights, some about me."

Cam stops and makes a face, adding, "Ray hated having me around. I know he wanted Bobbi to kick me out."

I feel my dislike for Ray growing.

Cam sighs and continues. "But Bobbi let me hang around, probably because by then I was doing all the cooking and cleaning and laundry. Then Ray got in some kind of trouble and he said we had to leave town. Bobbi quit her job and loaded her stuff into a trailer, along with Ray's stuff. I didn't want to leave with them, but I didn't know what else to do or where to go. We ended up at a motel a ways down the highway from here."

I try to picture the place she's talking about. "That place near the diner, with the busted-out sign?" I ask.

She nods.

"I didn't even think it was open."

"The old lady who owns it could hardly believe it when we stopped and said we wanted to check in."

"So that's where you were staying . . . with Ray and Bobbi?"

"Yeah, for the past few days." Cam takes a deep breath and says, "You want me to keep going?"

"Well, yeah. How did you get the cut on your head? How did you end up here?"

"All right. Here's what happened, okay? Ray has a collection of hubcaps." She rolls her green eyes. "And I saw a picture in an old magazine in the motel room of a bird feeder made out of a hubcap. I was bored so I took one lousy hubcap out of the trailer and was using some of his tools to poke holes in the edge so I could attach strings like in the picture, and Ray came outside and was mad because I ruined one of his stupid hubcaps. Then Bobbi came out and started hollering, too, saying she'd done me this huge favor and why was I provoking Ray. I said I didn't see what the big deal was and Ray said, 'I'll teach you to mouth off.' "

Cam makes another face. "Ray is very sensitive about people 'mouthing off' to him. So he grabbed the hubcap from me and swung it and it hit me in the head. Then he pushed me into the motel room. I heard a noise and it was his screw gun, and he screwed the door shut so I couldn't get out. And then he left in the car with Bobbi."

I have been standing and listening, nearly hypnotized by her story, and now I slowly sit down in the chair across from her at the kitchen table. My eyes never leave her face.

After a moment she continues. "I didn't know—or care—if they were ever coming back. But being locked in, it's—" She stops and looks down at her hands, which are twisting over and over on the tabletop.

"It's a horrible feeling," she goes on in a low voice. "So, there I was. There was no phone in that lousy motel room. Nobody else was crazy enough to be staying there. I thought about screaming, but the office is in the old lady's house, which is up the hill behind the motel, and she'd never have heard me. I tried to stay calm. My head was bleeding, so I tied a towel around it and finally it stopped. Then it got dark and I got scared and hungry. When morning came and they still weren't back, I banged and banged on the door, and finally I gave up on that and broke the window and climbed out. I cut my arms and legs doing that, and the effort made my head start to bleed again. When I got out, I started walking.

"I was afraid they'd come back before I could get away. I was also afraid somebody would see me and see I was hurt and call the cops. So I got off the highway and went into the woods, and then I found the trail. Once when I looked back, I saw Josie. I didn't see you, but I figured there was probably a person with the dog and I was afraid whoever it was would see me, and that's when I climbed the hill and hid in the cornfield."

"Wow," I mumble. "Why do you think they won't just let you go?"

"I bet Ray's afraid I'll tell someone what he did and get him in trouble."

Cam looks at me then and smiles, which is about the last thing you'd think she'd do after the terrible story she just told. She says, "Anyway, I'm glad it worked out this way."

"*What?*" I say, feeling, as I usually do with this girl, one step behind. "Why?"

"Because I met you."

I feel strangely pleased—and somewhat confused—by this remark.

"With you helping me to signal them, my parents will find me and I'll never have to see Ray or Bobbi again."

Before I can say anything, she points to the bag of Tootsie Rolls and her eyes fill with tears.

Now I'm really confused. I can't imagine why a half-eaten bag of candy would make a person cry.

After a minute she sniffles and says, "Thanks for the Tootsie Rolls. That's the nicest thing anybody's done for me since I've been on Earth."

That does it. When she says that, I know that I'm going to do whatever I can to help her. I don't know what to believe, but I understand suddenly how much she needs *somebody*. And I'm the only one around.

6

AT FIRST CAM HAD ACTED SO SURE OF HERSELF.
Bossy, even. But now, after telling that awful story, she
seems small and scared.

"Your parents . . ." I say. "They must be pretty worried about you."

"I'm sure they are," she says.

"How long has it been? Since you've been on Earth,
I mean."

"Three weeks," she pauses, "and three days. Which
means my parents will be coming back in four days."

"Why four days?"

"The moon will be full again in four days. And that's
the best time to make contact. The trouble is, they're
sure to return to the same place to look for me and now,
because of Ray, I won't be there. That's why I have to
make a signal, so they can find me."

So many questions are crowding into my brain it's

hard to know where to start. "Well, in the meantime, why don't we go to the police and tell them what Ray did to you? People can't just hit kids and lock them up and leave them."

Cam gives me a tired glance. "Owen, you're not thinking. I can't risk going to the police. They might find out who I am. Remember the soldiers? And the guns? I can't risk getting taken into custody by your government. They'd probably want to do tests on me and who knows what else? It could put my parents and everybody on my planet in danger. No way."

I can see her point.

"I just need four days, and I'll be out of here," Cam presses.

"Four days," I repeat. "It shouldn't be too hard to keep your secret for four days."

"And that gives us a little time," she says.

"For what?" I ask cautiously.

She smiles, and looks both shy and excited at the same time. "To plan how we're going to make the signal," she says, "and"—those strange green eyes of hers sparkle—"for me to talk you—and Josie, of course—into coming with us."

"*What?*" I ask incredulously.

Cam pats Josie and says, "You want to come, don't you, Josie?"

Josie lets out a sharp, happy bark.

"I knew she was highly intelligent," says Cam, "and this proves it."

Josie wags her tail, the traitor.

I remember Cam saying, "They like dogs." I wonder, would the aliens like *me*? But wait a second. The whole idea is crazy, and I start to say so, but Cam speaks first.

"You don't have to answer now. Sleep on it." She's quiet for a minute. Then she says, "What I'd really like to do is get cleaned up."

Suddenly she sounds really sad and tired. I say, "Okay."

We walk together to the edge of the hill. Josie and I go down and check the stream to make sure there isn't anybody there. Then I survey the trail in both directions and peer around inside the old mill. There's nobody in sight, so I look up to the top, where Cam has hidden herself behind a bush and is peering down at me, and I give her the all-clear sign.

She slides down and asks, "Can you whistle?"

I let out a sharp blast between my teeth, and Josie gives me a puzzled look, as if to say, *How can I come when I'm already here?* I scratch her ears and tell her she's a good dog.

Cam smiles and says, "Just do that to warn me if somebody's coming." She heads to the stream, and I pace back and forth, kicking stones and waiting. Every small sound startles me, and I keep whipping around, half expecting Ray to come up behind me. Each time, I wonder what I would do if Ray actually did show up. I have no idea.

It's weird: most days when Josie and I are on our

run, we don't see anyone else on the trail, except for the Dog People. Now all of a sudden the trail is like a major highway. First, four people come by on bikes. I don't whistle to warn Cam, because these are obviously serious bikers. They're wearing shiny, brightly colored, tight-fitting clothes, special shoes, and helmets. They pedal by with their heads down and I'm not sure they even notice *me*, so I figure they're no threat to her.

But then along comes a guy with a fishing rod, and he's peering through the underbrush and I can see he's trying to scope out what this stretch of the stream looks like, so I whistle real loud. He gives me a strange look because, once again, Josie is right there.

That look makes me nervous, so I say, "I'm calling my other dog."

"Oh yeah?" he asks, real friendly and interested. "What kind?"

Quickly I say, "Golden retriever."

"Nice dogs," he says with a nod. "I used to have one. I'll keep an eye out for it." He keeps walking.

After about ten more minutes, Cam returns from the stream, dressed in the clean T-shirt and the shorts I brought her. The shorts are too big, so she's also wearing the belt I brought. The bandage around her head is gone, and I see the cut has closed up. Her hair is dripping and her face, legs, and arms are clean. It's an improvement, for sure.

But those green eyes of hers show up more now.

They really are the greenest, glitteriest eyes I have ever seen. If a little kid drew an alien, it might have eyes like hers.

"Well, I'll see you tomorrow," she says. It's not a question.

I guess that means I should go, but it doesn't feel right to leave her alone, not with Ray out there somewhere, looking for her. "Listen," I say. "Why don't you come home with me? I could hide you, and my dad would never know. He works all the time, and he's pretty clueless, honest."

"No."

"I'm sure if I told him, he'd help."

Cam looks alarmed. "You promised you wouldn't tell anybody."

"All I'm saying is—"

She interrupts. "The only help I want is with making the signal, and you and I can do that ourselves, Owen. *Please?* We don't need anybody else. It's too risky."

I hesitate. I'm worried about Ray, but I don't want to tell her that and make her any more scared than she already is. She must think I'm still thinking about telling my dad because she adds, "Will your father believe I'm from another planet? Will he leave the police out of it, jump right in, and help us signal my parents?"

I consider this. Dad didn't share the fascination Mom and I had with life beyond Earth. He never came out and said he thought we were nuts or anything like that. But he didn't join in our discussions or watch the same movies or read the same books we did.

"No," I admit.

In a whisper she asks, "But *you* believe me. Don't you? I can tell."

I look into her eyes and take a deep breath. "Yeah," I say. "I believe you."

She looks so grateful I have to look away.

"Out of all the people on Earth who could have found me, it was *you*," she says wonderingly. "I don't believe for one minute that was a coincidence. It was meant to be. Now that you're on my side, I just know everything is going to work out."

I feel flattered, but a little shaken by her faith in me.

We're both quiet for a minute. Then Cam says, "Hey, Owen? What about your mom? You never mentioned her."

"Mom?" I say, taken by surprise. "She'd believe you, too, I think," I add slowly. "But she died. In a car accident."

"Oh. I'm sorry."

Neither of us speaks for a while.

"Was she nice?"

"She was great," I say.

Cam's eyes look far away for a minute. Then she smiles, but it's a sad smile. "You're lucky," she says.

This seems like an odd thing to say. I must have looked surprised because she adds quickly, "I don't mean lucky that she died. I mean lucky you had such a good mom."

Suddenly there's a big lump in my throat. I quickly change the subject. "Look, I don't like leaving you alone. Aren't you scared to stay here by yourself?"

"Yes," she says in a small voice. "But I'm more scared of Ray catching up with me before I can escape."

Then she surprises me again by smiling and asking, "You know the big wheat field up there?"

I nod.

"It's the perfect place to make the signal."

"Really? How come?"

Cam shakes her head. "It's too complicated to explain right now. If you can get the stuff we need and bring it here, it'll be easier just to show you."

I'm intrigued by the idea of building a signal for alien visitors, but does she think I have high-tech materials like that lying around the house? "What kind of stuff?" I ask cautiously.

"Fifty yards of clothesline," she says. "Or something a little thicker. A four-foot-long board, a hammer, some nails, and a long tape measure."

I stare at her in astonishment. "*That's* what you need to build a signal that will reach outer space?"

She laughs. "Yup."

"Okay," I say. "I get it. You're kidding, right? This whole thing—it's all a big joke."

Instantly, her expression changes and becomes serious. She looks me right in the eye and says earnestly,

"No, Owen. Honest. That's all we need. Just wait. You'll see."

I want to believe her, and when I look back into those eyes of hers, I do. I repeat the list of materials to make sure I've got it right. "I'll see what I can find," I say.

7

MY DAD COMES HOME THAT EVENING AROUND eight o'clock. He puts together a sandwich in the kitchen, then joins Josie and me in front of the TV.

"You already ate?" he asks.

I nod.

"I see we're all out of tuna, so I'm having tomato and cheese. It's not too bad with that spicy mustard on it. I guess I need to go to the store."

For once I'm glad my dad is such a haphazard shopper. There's not much chance he'll ever miss the food that I'll be taking to Cam.

I look at Dad and wonder what would happen if I told him about Cam. But I can't. I promised.

When a commercial comes on, Dad turns down the volume on the TV and says, "I saw on the calendar that you have your soccer physical tomorrow morning at nine-thirty."

"Oh, right," I say. "I forgot."

"You can ride your bike there, can't you?"

"Sure."

"And can you mow the lawn afterward? It's getting pretty long."

"Okay," I say. Our yard is a couple acres, so mowing it is not a quick job, but I don't mind doing it so much now that Dad lets me use the riding mower.

Cam is expecting me in the morning. We didn't agree on an exact time, so I figure I'll go see her as soon as my doctor's appointment is over. It shouldn't take too long. I'll mow the lawn later in the afternoon.

"Great," says Dad. "I think there's gas in the mower."

I nod, and with that our conversation comes to an end. Now that I have a secret to keep, I can see the advantages of not having a father who'd say something like, "So, Owen, tell me about your day." Tonight I'm grateful when Dad turns the volume back up on the TV and starts to watch.

I decide to go into the room that's going to be the den, if we ever get our act together and unpack everything, and look up campion in my guide to wildflowers. I find the carton marked "Field Guides" and bring the flower book back into the living room. It almost looks brand new. I never paid much attention to flowers before, I guess.

"Looking for anything special?" Dad asks.

"A flower I found on the trail today." Which is actually sort of true. I look through the index until I find "Campion" and turn to the page. Next to the picture is a description and the Latin name. Then it says, "Alien. Roadsides, waste places. June–Sept."

So, Cam knew what she was talking about. I look up "alien" in the glossary. It says, "Foreign, but successfully established in our area by man, or as an escape."

I figure "an escape" is a plant that somehow travels from its native home and manages to survive where it ends up.

And I see how her name is kind of perfect for a girl who got left on Earth by a spaceship. I think of her saying her name could have been a lot worse. Flipping through the book, I see she's right. Some of the names are horrible, and they sure don't sound like flowers.

I make a list of the best, most disgusting-sounding ones I can find, and when I get into bed I have a big grin plastered on my face.

oOo

In the morning, I rush like a madman to get to the doctor's office on time, then have to sit in the waiting room for forty-five minutes before I'm called in.

I meet Dr. Gupta, who checks me out and tells me I'm a "fine specimen," which is a good thing, I guess, although it makes me feel like an exhibit at a school science fair.

I'm pleased to learn that I've grown an inch and a half and gained almost ten pounds since the last time I was checked by my old doctor. The weight isn't flab, as far as I can tell, so it must be muscle. Best of all, I'm approved for team tryouts.

I leave the office and ride as quickly as I can through town and back up the highway to home, where I put some food and drinks for Cam in my pack. Josie and I stop at Mr. Powers's store for another bag of Tootsie Rolls.

After giving Josie a Slim Jim and me a jawbreaker, Mr. Powers turns the scanner down, looks at me, and says, "If you don't watch out, you'll rot your teeth eating all that candy. I'm proud to say I've still got all my choppers, which you'll have to admit is pretty good for an old coot like me." He opens his mouth wide to show me.

"That's good, Mr. Powers," I say. "Don't worry, the Tootsie Rolls aren't for me." As soon as the words are out of my mouth, I wish I could take them back. Before he can ask me who they *are* for, I say, "But, hey, what about these jawbreakers you give me all the time? Won't they rot my teeth, too?"

He eyes me from under his thick white brows. "You saying you don't want any more jawbreakers, is that it?"

"Oh, no. I was just—"

Mr. Powers interrupts with a roar of laughter, and I laugh, too, then make my escape to the trailhead.

Checking my watch, I see it's already almost noon. I

pedal faster, and when I finally get to the deserted house, Cam is nowhere in sight. My heart flutters as I think of Ray. I put the pack filled with food on the table and call, "Cam? Cam, I'm here."

No answer.

Oh man, oh man, oh man. Now my heart is racing like crazy, and I run through the kitchen and up the stairs with Josie behind me, and I'm imagining that I'm too late and Ray has come and taken Cam and—

I burst through the doorway of the room where I first found her sleeping and there she is, lying on the bed, her face turned to the wall.

"Cam?" I shout, filled with dread that she won't move.

But she does. She stirs, then hunches her shoulders and remains lying there, not looking at me.

I grab her shoulders and turn her over, afraid that, once again, I'll see blood on her face. But, no, thank goodness, her cut looks okay, better than yesterday, and I can see where she has put a fresh smear of first-aid cream on it. Those green eyes look up at me with no expression, but the rims look suspiciously red, as if she's been crying.

"Cam, what's the matter with you? Why didn't you answer me? You scared me half to death! I thought—"

"It's all right," she says in a dull voice. "You don't have to make excuses."

"What are you talking about?"

When she doesn't answer, I say, "You mean because I'm late? I didn't tell you yesterday because I forgot. I had a doctor's appointment this morning."

Cam sits up, very straight. "Of course you did."

She says this coolly and sarcastically. She might as well have said, *Any idiot can see you're lying.*

"I had a physical for soccer," I explain angrily.

She stands up, walks past me and down the stairs. Bewildered and angry, I follow her to the kitchen, where she busies herself unpacking the food I brought.

"It's okay," she says. "Thanks for this stuff. You've been a big help. You don't have to make excuses about wanting to ditch me."

"*Ditch you?* What are you talking about? I'm here, aren't I?"

Without looking at me, she holds up her hand, palm out, like a traffic cop. "It's okay. I'm used to looking out for myself."

"*Cam,*" I almost shout. "Would you listen to me? I'm not 'ditching' you." I pause, feeling completely furious with her. "There's other stuff I have to do, you know, besides helping you. I had a doctor's appointment and my dad told me I have to mow the lawn today."

She continues to examine the food and doesn't answer.

I sigh loudly. "Fine. Whatever. Don't believe me. I have to go do the lawn now. I probably won't make it back today, but I'll come tomorrow morning for sure, okay?"

No answer.

"Okay?" I repeat, loudly and impatiently. Josie barks with alarm, but Cam still doesn't answer.

"You really are a pain in the butt, you know that?" I turn and leave the house.

8

I BIKE ALONG FURIOUSLY. OKAY, SO CAM THINKS I'm ditching her. Fine. I *won't* go back. That'll serve her right! If that's what she thinks of me, that I'd go back on my promise to help her, the heck with her.

But then I realize that if I don't go back, she'll think she was right about me ditching her, even though I didn't even think of it until she accused me. Now I have to go back, to prove to her that she was wrong, even though she deserves to get ditched for acting like such a jerk.

She's got me. I'm so mad I've been pedaling like a maniac, and I look back to see Josie panting and falling behind. I stop, park my bike, and walk over to the stream with her while she takes a drink. I sit down on a rock, take off my sneakers, and cool my feet in the water. When she's had enough, Josie lies beside me and I rub her ears the way she likes.

This feels as good to me as it does to her. The stream feels good, too, and the rippling sound is soothing. Gradually, I feel my anger begin to fade. And while I can't put it into words exactly, maybe I understand why Cam acted so weird. Anyway, I put on my sneakers, get up, and pedal back to the foot of the hill. I climb it and walk across the yard and into the kitchen. Cam is sitting at the table, eating the crackers and cheese I brought.

I blurt out, "Bastard toadflax!"

I expect her to look puzzled or to laugh. But, as usual, Campion does something I don't expect. She crosses her arms over her chest and says, "Hoary puccoon."

I can't believe it. Not only wasn't she surprised, but she came right back with one of the other gross flower names I found in the field guide last night. I pull the list out of my pocket and pick another.

"Clammy Everlasting."

Quick as can be, she says, "Horny goatweed."

I'm amazed. I'm looking at my list, but she actually *knows* these names. I come out with my favorite. "Naked miterwort."

Saying it out loud cracks me up, and then we're both laughing our heads off.

When she can talk, Cam says, "Nipplewort."

This kills me.

After a minute she adds, "Don't forget mugwort, lousewort, and its close relative swollen bladderwort."

And we both lose it again. Finally, I scan the list, gasping for breath. "I think I'm out."

Campion smiles and says, "There are more, but we hit the highlights."

"Those are some *rude* names." I wipe my eyes.

She nods. "So," she says, "you did some homework."

I smile.

"Did you tell your father about me?" she asks then.

"No!" I answer. "Why?"

She shrugs. "I didn't think so. But I was trying to picture what you were doing last night. I guessed you were watching TV together."

I'd never considered that she might think about me when I was gone, or try to imagine what I was doing. "We were," I say. Inside, I'm thinking that if she's picturing a cozy scene with Dad and me chuckling about the show we're watching, after confiding in each other about how our days went, she's got the wrong family in her head.

"I said I wouldn't tell him about you, and I didn't. Besides, my dad and I—we don't—really talk."

She looks at me, waiting for me to go on, and I do. Maybe it's because of those amazing green eyes, which show nothing but interest. Anyway, I start telling her how it is with my father and me.

"I mean, we *talk*, like, 'pass the butter' or 'I'll be home at seven.' But that's pretty much it."

I pause, because it's hard to explain. "I guess you

could say that Dad and I are *careful* around each other since Mom died." I shrug. "I'm used to it. The truth is, Dad doesn't seem to have much to say. I mean, he goes to work and comes home and gets up and goes to work again. I swear, there is no way my life is going to end up like that."

Cam's glittery green eyes are on me, waiting for me to go on, but I don't want to talk about this anymore.

Cam breaks the silence. "Sorry about being weird before," she says quietly. "I got scared you weren't coming back and I—I really need you to help me."

"It's okay," I say. "But, listen. I promised Dad I'd mow the lawn, so I've really got to go." I make a face and add, "And I promised I'd help you. *Do you believe me?*"

She smiles. "Yeah."

"I'll see you tomorrow."

"Okay."

"And I'll bring the stuff to make the signal."

"Okay."

"And if I'm not here at the crack of dawn, it's because it might take me a while to find some of the stuff. *Okay*, Campion?"

She smiles again. "*Okay*, Nipplewort."

∞∞∞

At home I start on the lawn, but the mower runs out of gas after a couple minutes. The five-gallon can in the garage is empty, so I put it in my old wagon and drag it down the highway to Mr. Powers's gas pump to fill it up. Josie trots along beside me.

To my dismay, Ray's car—there's no mistaking that hideous piece of junk—is pulling away from the parking lot as I near the store. Instinctively, I try to hide my face, but he doesn't even look in my direction. I realize I'd been secretly hoping he'd given up on looking for Cam and gone far, far away.

As I trudge across the parking lot to the gas pump, I see a leather work glove lying on the ground. It's in pretty good shape, so I pick it up and put it in my pocket, pump gas into the red gas can, and go inside to pay.

"Hello, Mr. Powers," I say.

Without a word, he gets a Slim Jim from the jar, peels it open, and feeds it to Josie. Then he takes a jaw-breaker from the other jar. "You're sure you want this now?"

I nod, and he rolls it across the counter with a friendly smirk.

I take the glove from my pocket and place it on the counter. "I found this outside," I say. Then, thinking I might learn something about Ray, I add, "I thought that guy who just left might have dropped it."

Mr. Powers examines the glove and shakes his head. "Not his," he says without hesitation.

"How do you know?" I ask.

"This here's a *work* glove. *Used.*"

I look at him questioningly.

Mr. Powers snorts. "I'd lay odds that fella's never done an honest day's work in his life."

I laugh, then notice that Mr. Powers is scowling, probably at the thought of Ray. I wait, hoping he'll have more to say on the subject, but he doesn't. I don't want to appear too interested, so I don't ask if Ray mentioned the girl again. I hand over the money for the gas and Mr. Powers takes it.

"No Tootsie Rolls today?"

"Well, actually," I say, "now that you mention it, I think I will buy some. I'll take two bags."

He counts out my change, shaking his head and saying, "For a fella who doesn't eat 'em, you sure buy a lot of these things."

I give a nervous laugh and get the heck out of there before I say something stupid. On the way home I remind myself to be careful. Mr. Powers is old, but he doesn't miss much.

By the time I've finished mowing the entire yard, it's almost seven-thirty. Dad gets home as I'm putting the mower away. I worry that he's going to ask why I'm finishing up so late, but he doesn't. He just unpacks some ribs from a place called Sticky Fingers Bar-B-Q, and we get our plates and head for the living room.

I expect Dad to turn on the TV, but he says, "How was your doctor's appointment?"

"Okay. I got approved for soccer tryouts."

He nods. "Good."

There's a short silence, and Dad reaches for the remote.

∞∞

In the morning, I raid the kitchen again and gather the stuff Cam said we'd need. We don't have any clothesline or rope, but I do have a hammer, nails, and a tape measure. I even find the wooden board she asked for.

The first weekend after we moved here, Dad and I went to the home supply store to buy stuff to build a deck off the kitchen. He was pretty fired up about the idea then, but somehow the actual building of the deck kept getting postponed, along with the actual unpacking.

The eight-foot-long boards we bought are still lying in a pile under a blue tarp in the yard, and I pull one out. I figure it'll be a long time before Dad notices it's missing, if ever.

I take the brand-new circular saw out of the box, get an extension cord, and cut one of the boards in half, thinking how my old shop teacher, Mr. Weberly, would have a fit if he saw me doing this without safety glasses.

I put the other stuff in my backpack and use a couple of bungee cords to fasten the piece of wood onto the rack over my rear fender. Then I grab more of my allowance money, in case Mr. Powers has any clothesline for sale. My back tire looks low, and I know he has an air machine.

"Well, well, you and the hound are turning into my best customers." He gives Josie her Slim Jim, then asks, "What can I do for you?"

"Do you have any clothesline?"

"Nope," he says.

"Oh."

"Doing the laundry, are you?" he asks with a sly little smile.

I can't very well tell him I'm helping the girl I haven't seen build a signal for space aliens, so I just stand there like a dope while he looks at me curiously from under those eyebrows.

"Son?" he prompts.

"Well, if you don't have any . . ." I say, edging away from the counter.

"It'd help to know what you need it for."

My mind goes blank. I'm lousy at this.

Mr. Powers sighs, then points to the wall near the door. "A lot of folks use that rope over there to tie up their boats. Will that do for you?"

I walk over and examine the spools of line. The thinnest one looks like it might be okay. Again, I wish I'd asked Cam more questions. I hold it up. "How much does it cost?"

"I'll give you what's left on the spool for ten dollars," he says.

"Do you think there's fifty yards?" I ask.

He nods. "I'm giving you a bargain, by the way."

"Great. Thanks."

After I pay and he gives me my change, I ask, "Is it okay if I fill up my bike tire?"

He rolls a jawbreaker across the counter to me, winks, and says, "Air's still free, last I heard."

"Thanks."

He says, "Building something?"

"No," I answer, puzzled at the question. But then I realize he's looking at my bike with the board sticking out past my fender. I shrug and say, "No, it's just a board," which is right up there with the dumbest statements ever made.

Mr. Powers doesn't comment on this. He just nods thoughtfully and looks at me with those droopy eyes. Josie and I make our escape and go around to the back of the store where the air pump is.

9

RIDING DOWN THE TRAIL, CAREFULLY BALANCING my load, I sigh when I see that the Dog People are here again. And—I can't believe it—I think I see a new dog. Josie scoots right up to sit at the Dog Woman's feet and waits patiently for the treat she knows will come. Sure enough, it does.

"You are so polite and ladylike," the woman says to Josie. "Not like this bunch of hooligans we've got."

"Is that a new one?" I ask, pointing to a cute, medium-size brown mutt with floppy ears. All the other dogs are tearing around, having a wonderful time, but this one is standing close to the van and shivering. His tail is between his legs and he looks totally pathetic.

"Yes," says the woman. She makes a sad face. "That's Sidney. He's having a rough time. He must have been horribly mistreated. It's going to take a while, I think, before he trusts us."

"Where'd you get him?" I ask.

"Same place we get 'em all. The shelter called to say they had another dog nobody wanted."

The man joins us. "He'd have been put down if we hadn't taken him." To Sidney, he says, "We couldn't let that happen, could we, boy?"

Sidney's tail moves in a tentative wag, then tucks back between his legs.

"He'll come around once he settles in with us," the man says confidently. "We've had worse cases, haven't we, hon?"

The Dog Woman nods. "Lord, yes. Why, Simone over there was too terrified to leave her crate when we got her. It took us three days to coax her out. Now look at her."

She points to a big black dog leading a string of followers over to the stream, where they begin to splash and play.

I watch. My opinion of the Dog People is beginning to change. I ask, "Do you ever say no when the shelter calls? I mean, is there a limit to how many dogs you'll take?"

The Dog People look at each other and burst out laughing. The man says, "We've given up on setting limits. Every time we do, a dog comes along who really needs a home."

"How many do you have?" I can't help asking.

"Nineteen," the woman says. "We wanted kids, but

that wasn't meant to be. So we figure this is what we were put on earth to do instead."

"Lucky for them," I say, pointing to the pack.

"Oh, for us, too," the woman assures me. "They bring us a lot of joy. I can't imagine the two of us rattling around alone in our big, old house. We live just a quarter mile down the road. We have a small yard, so it's nice to have this trail nearby. These guys love to run."

I try to picture their house, and I imagine it looks like them, sort of shabby and messy and comfortable.

"Do you ever give any back?" I ask. "Like if they turn out to be troublemakers or something?"

The man and woman look at each other. "No," they say together, shaking their heads.

"We get attached," the woman adds. "And they get attached to us."

"Nineteen dogs," I murmur with wonder.

"Of course, there are the cats . . ." the man says.

"Cats?" I repeat.

The woman lets out a loud hoot. "Only seventeen of *them*!"

I'm revising my opinion again. These two *are* nutcases, the kind of people you see on the news with the police raiding their filthy house, which is filled with animals and animal poop.

"Wow," is all I can think of to say.

"When the city started tearing down the old

foundry building, they discovered fifteen cats living there. We already had two cats, but if we didn't take them . . . well, I don't have to tell you what would have happened to 'em."

"Wow," I say again. "Do they get along okay with the dogs?"

"For the most part," says the woman. "They seem to work it out."

"At least cats don't need to be walked," I say.

"Good thing for us."

"Well, we'd better get moving," says the woman. "These rascals need to work off some energy. We'll see you soon, Josie, and you, too . . ."

"Owen," I say.

"Hi, Owen. Glad to meet you. I'm Charlene."

"And I'm Ernie," the man says, holding out his hand.

We shake, and Charlene says, "Might as well be on a first-name basis, since we all seem to be regulars here."

As Josie and I head off I smile, thinking that it's nice to know Charlene and Ernie's names. It's better than thinking of them as the Dog People. Or the Dog-and-Cat People. Also, it's good to know they have all those critters because they're softhearted, not soft in the head.

Well, okay, maybe a little bit of both.

It takes two trips up the hill to carry all the stuff. Cam oohs and aahs and declares that everything is perfect, which makes me feel better about spending more of my allowance on her, and getting grilled by Mr. Powers.

We take a bag of Tootsie Rolls outside and sit on the edge of the porch, our legs dangling. Josie chases a squirrel up into a big sycamore tree, then comes back and curls up beside me, looking proud of a job well done.

"Good girl," I tell her. We watch as a breeze rises, making the leaves shudder. Clouds gather and soon block out the sun. After a while I ask Cam, "So now you've got to tell me. How is that stuff"—I gesture toward the pile of building materials—"going to make a signal to outer space?"

She laughs. "You've heard of crop circles, haven't you?"

"Of course," I say. Anybody interested in aliens and interplanetary travel has read about them. They're designs that mysteriously show up in fields of wheat or barley or oats. The crop is flattened out to make a pattern, which can only be seen from the air.

They're called crop *circles* even if they aren't circular. Some of them are made by hoaxers who want to trick people into thinking the circles were made by UFO's. But there are a lot of people who think that some of the circles really *were* made by spaceships landing and taking off. Others say the designs contain messages left by the alien visitors.

"Wow! Is that what we're going to make?"

Cam nods.

"How?"

She smiles. "You'll soon see."

"This is so cool!" I exclaim.

"I just worry about my parents. I wish they never had to set foot on Earth again."

This takes me by surprise. And I know it's dumb, but I feel personally insulted somehow. "Why? What's the matter with Earth?" I ask.

"Well, for starters, you know what happened when my parents' ship was spotted."

"You mean the jeeps and soldiers and guns?"

"The reception wasn't exactly what you'd call friendly."

"That's true," I admit.

"And just look around you," Cam says. "Earth has wars, hatred, pollution, greed, cruelty . . . all sorts of terrible things."

I frown. "You mean there's nothing like that on your planet?"

"Imagine a world where people are never cruel to children or"—she stops to kiss Josie's nose—"animals, or anyone."

"It sounds great," I say. "It's nice to think there's a place like that. I can see why you want to go back."

"I want so much for everything to go smoothly," Cam says, hugging her arms to her chest. "With luck, nobody but my parents will see our crop circle until after we're gone."

"What's it going to look like, anyhow?"

Cam goes inside and comes out with a scrap of paper and a pencil stub. When she's finished drawing, she passes the picture to me, and to tell the truth, I'm disappointed.

I'd been expecting something intricate and, well, *alien*-looking. This drawing shows a series of circles inside each other, like an archery target. Any little kid could draw it.

"What?" she says, examining my face, where I suppose my feelings must show.

"It's fine," I answer quickly. "It's just not what I imagined."

"It's pretty simple," she says. "But that's the whole idea. We have to make it in one afternoon, to lessen the chances of it being discovered."

"Do we just walk around in the field knocking down the wheat stalks in circles?" I ask. "We're not going to be able to see what we're doing. How will we know if we're getting way off course? We could end up sending the wrong signal, like ATTACK EARTH NOW!"

Josie jumps up and barks in alarm when I yell this. I laugh and pat her head.

Cam smiles and says, "It's okay, Josie. They would never do that, even if we did mess up and tell them to."

"The heck they wouldn't!" I exclaim. "That's what I've seen in movies anyway."

She shakes her head. "You have got a *lot* to learn about my planet."

"So tell me more," I challenge.

"Okay." She pauses for a second, like she's getting her thoughts together.

Suddenly I hear a car. "Listen!"

Cam freezes, a look of fear in her eyes. "Please," she whispers. "Don't let it be Ray."

"Come on!" I say. "Quick!" I grab the paper and pencil and Josie's collar and run toward the cornfield. I glance back and see that Cam is following. We duck into the field as a large white SUV with the words LAKELAND REALTY on the side comes up the driveway and stops in front of the house. A woman gets out, wearing a gray suit and high heels.

Cam and I exchange a glance of relief. It's not Ray. But, still, this is not good.

I hang on to Josie, who is trying to wriggle out of my grasp. "Shhh," I whisper, and clamp my free hand around her muzzle to keep her from barking.

The woman takes small, careful steps across the uneven gravel drive, climbs the stairs onto the porch, and stands for a minute looking at the door, which is wide open. She peers inside, but stays on the porch.

I picture the kitchen as we left it: food strewn across the table, the sweatshirt I'd brought Cam hung over the back of a chair, and the rope, hammer, nails, measuring tape, and board.

"Hello?" The woman's voice, sounding hesitant, carries across to where Cam, Josie, and I are hiding behind the first row of corn. "Is anybody there?"

She stands on the porch, looking frightened, then closes the door and glances around before heading quickly to her SUV. She gets in, and the instant the door is shut, I hear the sound of the automatic door locks clicking into place. The wheels send up a spray of small stones as the lady backs up and drives away, her cell phone already in her hand.

"I bet she's calling the county sheriff's office to tell them someone's been trespassing out here," I say. "From the way she ran off, she might even think somebody's in there now. The cops are going to be here soon, for sure."

Cam has dropped her face into her hands. At first I think she's crying, but then I see she's rubbing her eyes in an effort to concentrate. After a couple seconds, she looks up at me and says, "It would be best to leave everything in the kitchen just the way it is. So if that lady comes back with the sheriff, they'll think whoever was in the house is long gone, not still hanging around."

This makes sense, and I nod.

Then Cam looks up with a stricken expression. "But I've got to go back in and get the things for making the signal." She looks up at the sky. Dark clouds are moving in quickly. "Where can I go?" She thinks for a second, then asks, "What about that big abandoned building by the stream, near where I got cleaned up?"

"The mill? No way. People go in there all the time to look around. Kids hang out there and party."

After another moment she asks, "Do you have a tent?"

"Yeah," I answer. I know what's coming, of course. She wants the tent to sleep in tonight. I can't help being impressed by her calmness and her courage. She doesn't know where Ray is, or if he's still looking for her. But she is determined to hang on until the night of the full moon.

And I'm determined to help her.

"Do you think you could go get it while I clear my things out of the house?" she asks.

"Sure. I'll get the tent, if you want. But—" Thinking of Ray, I hesitate, then plunge ahead and ask again. "Why don't you just come home with me?"

She looks so alarmed, I quickly add, "I don't mean we tell my dad or anything. I really can hide you."

She shakes her head and says very quietly, "No. I can't take a chance of getting caught now. Not when I'm so close."

By now I know better than to argue. "Okay. I'll get the tent. First, I'll help you get the stuff out of the house. We've got to hurry, though. This place is way back off the road, but it's not all that far from town. The sheriff could get here in twenty minutes, if he wants to."

Quickly, we walk toward the house. Inside she says, "I'll just grab my—well, *your*—clothes. Can you get the board? I'll take the rest of this." She gathers up the signal-making tools and swipes the bag of Tootsie Rolls from the table. We take the stuff back to our hiding place in the corn.

"I'll be back as soon as I can," I promise. "We'll find some safe place to set up the tent."

And I begin yet another trip down the trail.

10

I PEDAL ALONG, AND A SUDDEN WIND PICKS UP. BIG, fat raindrops begin to fall, feeling like jelly beans pelting the bare skin of my arms and face. Soon I'm soaked, and even though it's July, I'm shivering like crazy. When I finally make it home, my teeth are actually chattering.

I look at Josie, whose short, thin coat is no protection from this kind of rain. She's drenched to the skin and is shaking as much as I am. I towel her off, rubbing hard to make her warm. Then I towel off my own hair and throw on some dry clothes. I get some dry clothes for Cam, too. Remembering that we left the food in the kitchen, I grab some beef jerky, crackers, cheese, and a couple cans of soda.

All the while, I'm picturing Cam huddled in the cornfield, drenched and freezing. I tell myself not to rush so much that I forget something important. I really don't want to make another trip back and forth today.

Out in the garage, I find the tent, rolled up in its carrying case. It's a two-person backpacking tent, very lightweight and compact, thank goodness, since I'll have to drag it up the hill. Next to it on the shelf is a tarp to use for a ground cloth, and two rolled-up sleeping bags. I take one. Then, thinking it could be a cold, wet night, I take the other as well, along with an old newspaper and a book of matches. I put everything into a big garbage bag and tie the top tight.

I notice that it's already after six o'clock. There's a chance Dad will be back before I am, so I scribble a quick note, saying I might be home late and he should eat without me.

Josie watches my every move, as always, and when I put on my rain slicker, she runs to the door, her tail wagging. I don't really feel like heading back outside, but Josie isn't about to let a little wet weather stop her.

"You sure you want to come, Josie?" I tease.

She barks and scrabbles her front paws on the floor in eagerness to get going.

"Okay," I say, laughing, and we step outside. I strap the stuffed garbage bag on my bike, and we head down the drive toward the highway. The wind has stopped, but the rain has settled into a steady downpour.

I pedal along, head bowed to keep the water out of my eyes, with Josie trotting alongside. As we near Mr. Powers's store, I remember seeing yellow rain ponchos for sale on a shelf by the door. I check the parking lot for Ray's car, and when I see no sign of it, I decide to get one for Cam, at the risk of arousing the old man's curiosity even more. I pull in and park my bike under the roof over the gas pump, and Josie and I go inside.

Mr. Powers looks up from his stool behind the register and turns down the police scanner, which is blaring as usual. He says, "It appears you don't know enough to stay in out of the rain, son."

"I'm in now," I say.

"So you are," he observes. As usual, he reaches into the jar of Slim Jims, peels one for Josie, and feeds it to her, calling her a "good little hound dog." He rolls a jawbreaker across the counter to me and says, "People are always complaining about kids today, how they don't do nothin' but sit in front of the TV or the computer screen. Far as I can tell, though, *you* don't hardly ever sit still. Back and forth, back and forth, a couple times every day. Got your bike all loaded up when you go *thataway*"—he jerks his thumb toward the trailhead—"but it's empty when you come *thisaway*"—he points to the highway heading toward my house. "I ask myself, what's that boy *doin'*?"

When I don't answer, he shrugs and says, "None of my business, of course."

He's right, but I don't think that's going to stop him, and it doesn't. He goes right on to say, "I got a lot of time on my hands between customers, you know, so I sit here all day listening to the scanner. A while back the sheriff got a report that somebody was in the house on the old Davie place, might be living in there."

He's not asking a question, so I don't answer, but he just keeps looking at me, and as the silence grows between us, I start to feel desperate to break it. "The old Davie place?" I repeat. To my annoyance, my voice comes out sounding squeaky. "Where's that?"

He grins, and I feel like I'm the mouse in a game of cat and mouse. "Right off that trail you head for every day," he says. "Walt Christensen's farming the place since old man Davie died and his wife went into the home."

I don't know any of the people he's talking about, and I say so.

"But you know the place?" he persists. "Old farmhouse, up that way." He pauses, then adds, "I expect you can't see it from down there on the trail."

I shake my head, playing dumb.

"Well, see, here's what got me thinking," Mr. Powers goes on. "I watch you going up that way all the time. And that big-neck fella keeps coming in, asking about a missing girl. He came back again today—"

"What?" I'm too freaked by this news to pretend to act cool. "He came back?"

Mr. Powers nods, looking pleased at my reaction. "Yessir. About a half hour ago. In that car of his, the one looks like it got shot but didn't die."

My heart plummets.

"Scanner was on, naturally, and that fella seemed

mighty interested in the news. Asked me where was this Davie place."

He stares at me from under his eyebrows.

"Did you tell him?" I ask.

"You kidding?" says Mr. Powers with a snort. "Guy like that? I wouldn't give him change for a nickel if he gave me a dollar."

I take a deep breath and tell myself to settle down.

Mr. Powers continues to eyeball me and says, "Now here's you, acting jumpier than a sack of fleas. I put it all together, and I gotta wonder what's the connection, you know what I mean?"

I try to act unconcerned. "Beats me. I sure don't know that guy. Anyhow, I better get going."

He studies me. "You didn't come in to buy something?"

I stop. *Darn him.*

"Just stopped in to chat with an old man, did you?" he goes on.

I think about the poncho for Cam and decide it is too big of a risk. "That's right, Mr. Powers," I say. "Just stopped in to say hi and get out of the rain for a minute. I'll be seeing you."

"And I'll be seeing *you*," he says with a grin and a lift of his white caterpillar eyebrows.

I hardly even notice the rain as I pedal furiously down the trail. Ray heard the police report of someone living in a deserted farmhouse nearby. He asked where the house was.

Could he have already found it somehow? *Found Cam?*

I pedal faster, unable to shake a feeling of impending disaster. I feel as if Cam and I are being closed in on from all sides.

When I finally get to the hill and start climbing, the loose shale is super slippery from the rain, and I nearly kill myself trying to get up with all the stuff I've brought. I drag myself to the top and peer over the edge, half expecting to see Ray leering back at me. Instead, there's a sheriff's patrol car parked in the driveway of the farmhouse.

I slide back down the bank and let the bag in my hands tumble down on its own. I sit at the bottom of the hill for a minute, feeling tired and discouraged. Josie licks my face anxiously. I get up and make a run for the old sawmill, dragging the bag with me. The mill is right on the trail, and never seemed sinister when I passed it in the daylight. But now, in the duskiness of the rainy evening, it feels spooky. At least it's a roof over our heads while we wait for the sheriff to leave.

The mill is just a shell now; the windows are gone and so are the doors. The brick walls are damp and mossy, with dumb graffiti painted on them. The cement floor is strewn with leaves and sticks and dirt, along with beer cans and food wrappers left by kids, and the ashy remains of a fire.

It's dank and gloomy in here, and I feel my spirits sink even further as I sit leaning against a giant, rusty iron gear that was part of the millwork. Josie sniffs around for a while, then comes and lies in front of me, her head on my legs. I reach down and stroke her velvety ears, glad for her warmth and easy company.

When I figure the sheriff has satisfied himself that whoever was in the house is gone, I make my way up the hill again. No cars, that's good. I see that the door is boarded shut and there is now a sign posted on it: NO TRESPASSING BY ORDER OF YATES COUNTY SHERIFF. Somehow that, along with the rain and general gloom of the early evening, makes the place look sadder and more deserted than before.

I scan the area for a good place to set up the tent. Unfortunately, the nylon is a bright orange color, so we're going to have to be really careful. After I've stood there for a couple seconds, Cam comes out of the cornfield and walks toward me, her plastic bag of stuff in her arms. When she gets close, she gives me a brave smile, but I see that her arms and legs are covered in goose bumps and her lips are blue and shaking.

"Listen," I say. "Ray came back to the store. They were talking on the scanner about someone possibly living in a deserted house nearby, and Ray was real interested. He asked Mr. Powers where the house is. Mr. Powers didn't tell him, but—"

"But he could find out from somebody else," Cam finishes, her green eyes wide with apprehension.

"So if you won't come home with me—"

She shakes her head quickly, sending drops of water flying from her soaking hair.

"Then we've got to hide the tent really well," I say. I point to a huge sycamore on the edge of the woods, where the trees meet the corn. It's about as far away as the length of a soccer field. "It'll be drier under that tree. I'm thinking that with rain this hard, Ray would have to be crazy to come way out here."

Cam looks worried, and I try to reassure her. "We'll move to a more hidden spot tomorrow. It's going to be dark before we know it, and you've got to get under cover and get warm."

She nods. I head for the tree and she follows. I was right: it is drier under the canopy. From there we can see only the very top of the farmhouse chimney, so there's no way someone at the house could see us. This is as safe as we're going to get tonight. I spread out the ground cloth, then take the tent out of the trash bag and unfold it, trying to remember how to set it up.

There are a lot of short metal pieces we have to fit together to make poles. Then we have to figure out how the poles fit through the nylon loops and tunnels. We fumble around, getting it wrong. Finally, when everything falls into place, the tent pops up like magic.

"Piece of cake," I mutter with relief. To Cam I say, "Okay, get in there and change into some dry clothes. And wrap yourself in the sleeping bags. I'm going to make a fire."

"Are you sure?" Cam asks. "It seems risky."

Her teeth are chattering and Josie is drenched to the skin again. "There's more risk of you and Josie getting hypothermia than of a small fire being seen," I tell her. I try to get Josie to go into the tent with Cam, but she seems determined to stay with me.

My friend Kevin and his dad were in scouting together since Kevin was a little kid, and I went camping with them once. Even though it was raining, Kevin's dad insisted that we needed a campfire. He knew all about building fires, even without matches, and even in the rain. He taught us that the branches of spruce trees shed water like an umbrella, leaving the ground almost completely dry underneath.

So I head for the spruce on the hillside and find some dry cones and twigs underneath. Then I break off a couple slightly larger dead branches, and some a bit larger than those. A few feet away from the tent, I carefully crumple the sheets of newspaper I've brought, and place the small, dry twigs and spruce cones on top. Then I light the paper. After several tries, the small twigs catch, and I slowly add bigger and bigger sticks.

To my relief, the rain has begun to let up, turning from a downpour into a slow, steady drizzle. I think I might actually be able to keep this fire going. The wind has died down, too, so I don't have to worry too much about setting the tent ablaze.

Cam has changed and wrapped herself in one of the sleeping bags, and is peering out the tent flap at the fire with a look of amazement. "How did you do that?" she asks.

I shrug modestly. "Shove over. Josie's cold."

"Come on in here, Josie," Cam urges, patting the sleeping bag beside her.

Josie whines and looks from me to Cam and back at me. I laugh.

"Looks like she's not coming without me," I say.

"There's plenty of room," says Cam, wiggling sideways.

I take off my slicker, crawl in, and wrap myself in the other sleeping bag. Josie jumps in right behind me and shakes herself all over. Cam and I both groan, then start to laugh as Josie circles a few times and plops down between us and happily starts licking herself dry.

From my bundle, I take out the cheese, beef jerky, and crackers. Cam holds up the bag of Tootsie Rolls she brought from the farmhouse and smiles.

"I know, I know," I say. "Tootsie Rolls first, dinner later. That's the way you aliens do it."

"Careful who you call an alien," Cam says, ripping the bag open. "Where I'm from, *you're* the alien."

"Speaking of that," I say, "you invited me to go back 'home' with you, but you still haven't told me much about what it's like there."

"True," says Cam. "Before I tell you, let's get comfortable. I want to watch the fire." She wriggles around so her head is at the tent's doorway and rolls over on her stomach. "That's better."

I do the same thing, and we lie on our bellies with Josie between us, gazing into the flames, which are holding their own against the drizzle.

Cam sighs. "This is nice," she says.

It is. Now that we're dry and warm, it's fun listening to the rain on the tent and looking into the misty gloom outside the glow from the fire. It's like we're in our own cozy world. The odor of wet dog mixes with smoke and chocolate and all the damp, piney, wormy smells of the outdoors.

Even with all the crazy things that are going on, I feel happier than I have for a long time.

11

WE LIE FOR A WHILE IN COMPANIONABLE SILENCE.
Then Cam says contentedly, "Earth definitely has its
strong points. In some ways, I'm going to hate to leave.
Especially since I've met you. That's why I really hope
you'll come."

I feel my cheeks growing red. I hope Cam can't see,
or else that she'll think it's because of the fire.

"We've been so busy hiding and getting supplies and
worrying about Ray, you haven't told me too much
about where I'm going," I say. Then I add quickly, "If
I'm going anywhere."

"Believe me, the more you hear, the more you'll
want to come with us. So what do you want to know?"

"Everything," I say, and settle in to listen.

"Okay, but first," Cam begins, "I just want to say
I'm not dumping on Earth, or anything like that, okay?"

"Okay," I say.

"Because I thought you got a little mad when I said my people aren't too crazy about coming here . . ." She looks at me with a question in her eyes.

"Yeah, that was dumb," I say. "I mean, Earth isn't perfect, that's for sure."

"Okay, good. Because the thing is, my planet started out the same way Earth did, but it ended up evolving differently. And, like I was telling you before, my people have almost stopped trying to make contact with Earth. Coming here is just too dangerous."

"Yeah," I say. "That's why you're worried about your parents coming back to get you."

She grimaces. "Yes. But of course they'll be willing to take the chance. I have a feeling . . ." Her voice trails off for a second. "Promise you won't laugh?"

"Promise."

"Well, I feel like you bring me good luck."

I laugh. "That's me. A real charm."

"Seriously," she goes on. "I could never have gotten this far on my own."

"I don't know about that," I say.

"I do," she says firmly. "I knew that first morning when you came to the farmhouse. I thought, *This is my chance.*"

We sit in silence for a minute. "Hang on to Josie," I say, and I get out of the tent to add more wood to the fire. The early darkness of a rainy night is falling fast, and I check my watch. It's past eight o'clock. Dad could be home by now, and if he is, he's going to be wondering where I am. I check to see if my cell phone works, but there's still no signal.

I don't feel like leaving yet. It's so wet and cold out, and so nice and warm in the tent by the fire, and I want to hear more about Cam's planet. I crawl back inside and break off a piece of cheese for me and one for Josie.

"So," I say, chewing, "tell me more." I wriggle into a more comfortable position, gaze at the fire, and wait.

Cam begins talking in a very soft, slow voice. "Well, people there—"

I can't help interrupting to ask, "Are they all like you? I mean, you seem to be, you know, a normal"—I hesitate—"*Earthling.*"

She laughs. "Thanks. I think." Then she continues. "Yeah, people there look like people here, pretty much. There are small differences, like in skin and hair and eye colors but you have to really look to notice them."

"Like your eyes," I blurt out, without thinking. "So green and glittery."

She seems surprised, then smiles. "Yeah. I've noticed that people here always remark about my eyes. Anyway, we evolved along with Earth for a long time, so we have a lot in common. Our two planets were really similar until we had a big war, kind of like your First World War."

I nod. It's not hard to imagine that.

"It was awful. But what came out of it, finally, was what we call the New World. That's the world I grew up in."

I'm concentrating on her words, trying to keep up.

"Home would be like Earth, except, well, we learned from our mistakes."

"And we didn't?" I ask.

Cam shrugs. "Listen to the news."

I say, "Most people here *try* to be good . . ." I hesitate, thinking of all the terrible stuff we hear about on the news. "Don't they?"

Cam says, "All I know is that kids on my planet are never unwanted. They don't have to be afraid."

I can hear in her voice that she's trying not to cry, and I feel awful. I think her time on Earth must have been really terrible.

Cam gazes directly into my eyes and says, "Kids on my planet aren't lonely, either."

"What are you looking at *me* for?"

She doesn't answer for a minute, but just keeps looking at me. Then she whispers, "That's one reason I thought maybe you'd come with me."

"What? You think *I'm* lonely?"

She looks flustered, and hesitates before saying, "I— I was thinking about what you said about your mom dying, and how your dad and you don't talk. And it doesn't seem like there's anybody else . . . I don't know, I could be wrong. But don't you just feel there's got to be some better place out there somewhere?"

I don't know what to say.

After a second, Cam adds, "I understand if you don't

want to leave here. I mean, this is the life you know. And your dad—"

"Oh, man," I say, interrupting, "speaking of my dad, he's probably starting to freak. I told him I might be late, but I've never stayed out *this* late." I untangle myself from the sleeping bag. "I gotta go."

Cam nods.

It's hard to leave the warmth of the tent to go into the darkness and rain. I step out and Josie rouses herself and follows. I turn back to Cam. She looks so alone and vulnerable in the tent by herself, it makes my heart twist up.

"I *really* have to go," I say.

"I know."

"I'll come back early and we'll move the tent somewhere safer," I tell her.

"Okay."

"Okay. Bye, then."

"Owen?"

"Yeah?"

"Will you think about it?"

"What?" I ask, although I know.

"Coming with me."

"Oh," I say. "Sure." How could I *not* think about it? What kid wouldn't want to take a ride on a spaceship? Who wouldn't want to live on the kind of planet Cam had described? I turn to leave, but she goes on.

"You know what's weird, though? Now, when it

looks like I'm actually going home, I suddenly have a reason to stay."

She says this and looks at me, and I think maybe she's talking about *me*, but I'm not sure, and I don't know what to say to that, if it's true. So I say, a little desperately, "I *really* have to go, Cam."

"I know."

I turn from the fire and at first I can't see anything. "Hey, by the way," I say, looking back. "What's the name of your planet?"

She blinks and looks surprised. After a second she says, "We just call it . . . Home."

"Oh. Okay."

This time I actually do leave. Sliding down the hill is pretty hairy in the dark. And once I'm riding down the trail, nothing looks familiar, and I wish I had a light on my bike. I don't feel sure of how far I've gone and how far I still have to go. I keep thinking I hear things—footsteps or movement—under the dripping of the rain. I'm really, really grateful for Josie's company.

Over and over, I tell myself that no matter how big and mean Ray is, there's no way he'd be out here on a night like this, and that the tent is well hidden, and Cam is safe.

12

BY THE TIME I PEDAL UP OUR DRIVEWAY, I FEEL SO exhausted I wonder if I'll be able to make it to my room and my bed. I notice that the house looks different, but it takes a minute for me to figure out why. Lights are on all over the place. This is strange, because Dad is a stickler for conservation—of energy and money. It's not a good sign.

Sure enough, as I'm stashing my bike in the garage, the door from the kitchen opens and Dad is standing there.

"Why haven't you been answering your phone?"

Josie goes up to him on a peacemaking mission, her tail wagging, but he ignores her and keeps looking at me.

"And what in the world were you doing out in this weather?" he continues before I have a chance to say anything.

I'm so beat I can hardly think, but I have to come up

with something. "I was on the trail. When it started to rain, I holed up in the abandoned mill I've told you about, waiting for it to stop, but it didn't. I tried to call then, but there's no reception down there so I turned off the phone. Finally, I just came home."

Dad looks puzzled. "When did you leave me the note?"

"Around six, I guess."

"It was already raining hard then. What was so important that you had to go out in it?"

My brain scrambles frantically for something to say. Lying seems like my only choice.

"I had some money in my pocket this morning and when I got home, it was gone. I figured it fell out on the trail, so I went back to see if I could find it."

He nods, and I silently congratulate myself for coming up with a reason he would understand. "Any luck?" he asks.

I make a face. "Nope."

"That's too bad. But, Owen, you really had me worried. I don't want you out at night like this, especially when I have no idea where you are."

"Sorry, Dad."

I follow him, blinking, into the brightly lit kitchen. In spite of the snacks I ate in the tent with Cam, I am suddenly ravenous, and I open the refrigerator.

Dad says, "I bought two steaks. Yours is in there. Here, give it to me. I'll cook it."

"Thanks," I say, handing him the plastic-wrapped

meat. He heats up the frying pan and asks me to get the butter. When it hits the pan, my stomach lets out a loud growl, and we both laugh. After that, the usual silence falls between us.

I fill Josie's water dish and put some extra food in her bowl, figuring she's burning up a lot of energy on the trail. Then I sit down at the table, watching Dad's back as he stands at the stove.

"Dad?" I say. "Are you ever . . . lonely?"

I can see from the way he stiffens that my question has startled him.

After a minute he says carefully, "I'm not sure what you mean."

Oh, boy. This is new territory. I wish I'd never brought it up. But then I flounder on. "I don't know. I mean, since Mom died."

Dad continues cooking my steak, and just when I think he's not going to answer, he says, "I don't think about being lonely. I think about my clients and what's going on in the world and what to pick up for dinner. And I think about you, of course."

"Oh," I say after a minute.

Dad puts the pan on the tile floor for Josie to lick. She circles it and sniffs, then lies next to it to wait for it to cool.

"Smart dog," says Dad.

"The smartest," I say.

He brings my plate to the table, sets it in front of me, and sits down.

"Are you okay?" he asks.

"Yeah."

"What you need is a hot shower and a good night's sleep," he says.

"Yeah," I say. "I'm really tired." I eat my steak. The sound of my chewing seems very loud in the quiet kitchen.

Josie has apparently determined that the pan is cool enough, because she stands up. The rhythmic lapping of her tongue fills the silence.

When I finish my steak, Dad takes my plate and washes it. For some reason this almost makes me cry.

I have the sudden thought that Dad and I are like two planets spinning in separate orbits, and that an unexpected little wobble just caused our paths to intersect for a moment. I feel like I want to stop everything before we spin off in different directions again, but I don't know how.

And I'm so tired, way too tired to think about it now.

13

THE NEXT MORNING, DAD HAS ALREADY LEFT FOR work when I get up. But there's a note on the kitchen counter.

> Owen,
>   I'm still working on that big audit, but I'm going to try to get home early tonight. Maybe we can talk some more.
>
>   Dad

I read the note over several times, shaking my head about how strange life can be. For the first time ever, Dad wants to talk? I mean, I'm glad. But why does it have to happen just when I'm up to my eyeballs in something I'm sworn to secrecy about, and just when I'm more or less counting on his being too busy and distracted to pay attention to me?

I don't leave him a note, because I figure I'll be back before he is. It shouldn't take all day to move the tent somewhere safer, and I'll be home in plenty of time to keep him from worrying and asking questions.

I'm glad to see the sun is shining. The water from last night's downpour is evaporating off the fields around our house and rising in a shimmery mist. It's pretty, and I smile, remembering Cam's comment that Earth isn't all bad.

I feed Josie, then start to make breakfast. Thinking that Cam is probably hungry after her rainy night alone in the tent, I make four fried egg and ham sandwiches on English muffins. I eat one, and wrap the rest in aluminum foil and put them in my backpack, along with some other food and drinks to get her through the day.

Then Josie and I head out. I'm glad not to have a reason to stop at the store, but I imagine Mr. Powers's droopy eyes on me as I pass by. A little way down the trail, I see the Dog People, or, rather, their dogs, all racing toward me.

Then Charlene and Ernie appear, calling, "Pierre! Simone! Jasper! Come!" The dogs ignore them and start roughhousing with Josie.

"Hello, Josie!" Charlene says. "Hi, Owen!"

"Hi," I say, stopping and straddling my bike.

Charlene gives Josie a treat and says, "What a glorious day. Especially after that gully washer we had last night. You weren't out in that, were you?"

"Yeah," I say. "Actually, I was."

"You poor thing," she says sympathetically. She looks at me, and I notice that her eyes are bright blue. Not icy blue, but warm and bright like this morning's sky. They crinkle up at the corners when she smiles, which she is doing now as she watches the dogs. I've never really looked at her face before. It's nice.

The dogs have stopped playing and are gathered around me with their noses going a mile a minute.

"I'm going to take a wild guess that there's food in your backpack," Ernie says.

I laugh. "Yeah. Sandwiches. Still warm, too. I bet they smell great to these guys."

Charlene says, "I would *love* to have a dog's nose, just for one day, to see how the world smells to them. Can you imagine all the information they get that we don't even notice?"

I glance at Josie and Pierre, who are sniffing each other's butts with great concentration. I grin and say, "I think I could live without some of that information."

Charlene lets out a whoop, which causes Pierre and Josie to glance at her inquisitively, then go back to what they were doing.

"I'm with you on that, Owen," Ernie agrees.

"I'd still like to have the nose, just for a while," declares Charlene, adding, "but I'd use it with more discretion than those two." To me she says, "So are you going on a picnic?"

"Uh, yeah, I guess," I mumble. "Sort of."

"All by your lonesome?"

I shrug and say, "Well, me and Josie." To change the subject I ask, "Is that Sidney?"

Ernie nods, beaming proudly. "Can you believe it?"

I can't. He barely resembles the dog I'd seen cowering and shivering by the van. He's standing by Charlene's side, his head up, and his tail wagging.

"Wow," I say. "He's doing great."

Ernie leans down to give Sidney a pat. "We thought it might take longer for him to come around. But he seems to know he's safe now."

"When I think of what he must have gone through, it makes me so sad," Charlene says. "All he needed was kindness and attention."

I give Sidney a pat, too. "Well, I should get going," I say. "I'll probably see you soon."

"I sure hope so," Charlene answers. "You two have fun now."

I call to Josie, and we head off. Some of the other dogs follow us for a while, but eventually they turn back.

When I get near where the tent was last night, it's nowhere to be seen. I panic as images of Cam being discovered by Ray run through my mind. But then a figure drops down out of the branches of the big sycamore tree, and I breathe a sigh of relief.

"You scared me for a second," I call.

Cam grins and says, "Yeah, I could tell. What took you so long?"

I reach into my backpack and hold up the sand-wiches. "I was preparing a gourmet feast."

"Excellent!" says Cam. "I was about to start eating leaves and bark."

"What happened to the Tootsie Rolls?" I tease.

"I don't have a watch, but I bet they only lasted five minutes after you left last night," she says.

"Where's the tent?"

She points to the cornfield. "I took it down and hid everything. I even spread the ashes from the fire around and sprinkled leaves over the ground." She grimaces. "I guess I'm getting paranoid."

"Good thing we only have"—I stop and think—"wow! Only one more day, right?"

Cam nods. "Yep, one more day until the full moon. Hey, was your dad mad last night?"

"Not really. More worried than mad. But he wants me home early tonight, so we'd better get going."

"First, food," says Cam.

We sit in the grass, close to the cornfield in case we have to hide, and eat.

"I found a good place for the tent," Cam says. "Come on." I walk with her over to the edge of the bank and look down. Here, the shale slopes gently down to a level area, making a kind of step in the hillside, before it drops off more sharply above the trail. "I sat there," she says, "and I'm sure no one on the trail would be able to look up and see it. And someone would have to walk right to the edge of the bank and peer over to see it from up here."

After we finish eating, I check it out. She's right. It's a good spot. So we set up the tent and put her stuff inside, except for the four-foot-long board, which we leave out.

When we're all done and feeling as safe as possible, I say, "So, tomorrow afternoon we'll make the signal. Then what?"

"That's up to you."

"Up to *me*?"

"Well, tomorrow night I'm going to wait in the center of the circle for my parents, and when they come I'm going home with them. The only question is, will you and Josie be with us?"

I avoid the question by asking one of my own. "How can you be so sure your parents will want me to come? I *am* a degenerate Earthling, after all."

I'm only partly kidding when I say this. It would be just my luck to go to another planet only to discover that everybody there thinks I'm the equivalent of a Neanderthal.

Cam says, "*Of course* they'll want you. First of all, the very fact that you're with me will let them know you're okay. But, really, Owen, you've got to believe me. They wouldn't want you to live like this."

"Live like *what*?" I ask indignantly. She makes it sound like I'm holed up in a cave gnawing on bones.

Cam looks away. "So alone."

"What are you talking about, *alone?*" I protest. "I just moved here. How am I supposed to know anybody until school starts?" She doesn't say anything, and I go on. "Oh, I know. You're talking about me and Dad. Well, for your information, when I got home last night he cooked me a great dinner, and we sat down and had a real good talk."

This is a slight exaggeration, of course. But it *was* a good talk, for us.

"And he left me a note this morning, saying he's going to come home early tonight so we can talk some more and do something together, maybe practice some soccer moves or something."

The last part isn't strictly true, either, but I feel pretty sure that's what Dad was thinking when he wrote the note.

"That's good," Cam says softly.

"Look," I say shortly, "I've got to go." I take the rest of the food out of my backpack and push it over toward her. "Be careful. You should be okay if you stay hidden."

"Yeah," she says. "I'll be careful." Her voice is barely above a whisper, and she seems distant and sad all of a sudden.

"All right," I say, trying to sound a little less abrupt. "I'll see you tomorrow. We'll build the signal."

Josie jumps up and barks, ready to go if I am. And I am. I want to get away from Cam and her nosy comments about my life. What does she know about me, anyway? She can be really annoying sometimes.

14

WHEN I GET HOME, IT'S ONLY A LITTLE AFTER TWO. I've been so busy with Cam, it feels odd to have free time on my hands. I think about Dad coming home early, and decide to do something to surprise him.

I get out the weed whacker and trim the edges of the lawn. This is a noisy, boring chore that I avoid whenever possible, and Dad usually has to remind me three or four times. Josie doesn't like the racket, either, and takes refuge under the porch until I'm finished.

As I survey my handiwork, I see my soccer ball lying in the grass next to the pile of lumber for the abandoned deck project, and I get an idea. I'll build a goal in the yard, and tonight Dad and I will practice taking shots, just like I told Cam we were going to do.

I'm pretty excited as I pull out three of the boards from under the tarp and drag them into the garage. I get out the saw again and cut one of them in half. Then I nail the two short boards onto the ends of the longer boards to form a rectangle. I get two more boards, cut each of them in half, and nail them to the base of the frame in a triangular shape. Cool! The goal stands on its own, ready for action. It doesn't look like much and isn't regulation size, but that's okay. It'll serve the purpose.

I set it up at the edge of the lawn and take a few shots. This isn't easy, as Josie seems to think I've devised this exercise solely for her benefit. She chases after the ball trying to bite it, and when that doesn't work, she noses it along in front of her and pushes it with her paws. To her, the object of this fun new game is to keep the ball away from me. I figure it could actually be good practice to try to steal the ball from her, and I go after it, using my fanciest footwork.

We play for a pretty long time, until I've gotten a couple shots through the goal. I'm sweating like crazy and Josie and I are both panting, and I collapse on the grass. Josie comes over and flops down beside me, heaving, her tongue hanging out.

I lie there, picturing Dad's face when he sees the goal. He's going to be amazed. I check my watch. Quarter after four. I wonder how early he might be home. It's possible it could be any minute. We'll have time for some soccer before dinner. Afterward, we'll sit on the porch and shoot the breeze.

I look at my watch again. Twenty after four. I've got to do something to pass the time, or I'll drive myself crazy. When Dad told my new school that I'd be coming in the fall, they gave him a list of books my class was supposed to read over the summer. I have a couple of them in my room, and I look them over. One has a picture of a kid catching a baseball on the front, so I grab it and settle in on a lawn chair in the shade. Josie curls up on the grass beside me and falls asleep immediately, snoring softly.

The book is funny, even though the kid who is the main character loses his hand in a meat grinder in the first chapter, and when I look at my watch again I'm surprised to see that it's five-thirty. My stomach growls, and I decide to check the refrigerator.

There's a package of hamburger meat and a bag of buns, so I go back outside and put some charcoal on the grill, squirt it with starter, and light it. I always get a thrill—and a little bit of a scare—when it catches with that whooshing sound. It takes a while for the stinky stuff to burn off and for the coals to get to just the right temperature, and I figure the grill will be all set to go by the time Dad gets home. I make four hamburger patties and set them on a plate.

Then, thinking I'll *really* surprise Dad, I make a salad. I get out plates, forks, napkins, ketchup, mustard, a bottle of dressing, the works.

I go back outside to read some more, but it's harder to concentrate now that Dad will be home any minute. Every time a car goes by, I look up to see if it's turning into our driveway.

At six-thirty, the coals in the grill are almost burned

down to nothing, so I add more. By seven, I'm too hungry to wait any more, and I'm starting to feel grouchy, and ticked off at Dad. Why did he leave a note saying he'd be home early if he wasn't going to be?

I eye the telephone. He gave me grief for not calling him last night, so why doesn't he call me if he's not going to make it home early? I'm sure not going to call *him*.

I cook myself two cheeseburgers and eat quickly, standing at the kitchen counter, barely even tasting what I'm chewing. Josie watches, not begging, but on the alert for any bits that might fall to the floor. I give her the last bite of my second burger, and we go back outside.

I read until it starts to get too dark to see, then I sit staring blankly out at the neighbor's farm fields, feeling stupid. Did I really think things were going to be different with Dad, just because he was worried about me last night?

Josie climbs up onto my lap, and her warmth feels good in the evening chill. I look up at the sky and watch as one star after another appears. I think of Cam's planet and imagine her parents, worried sick and missing her, waiting for the full moon and the signal.

The stars become blurry as my eyes fill with a sudden wash of tears. I hug Josie fiercely, burying my nose in the familiar smell of her neck, recognizing that Cam was right. Except for Josie, I *am* alone. My mother's gone and I can't even remember her face clearly anymore. My father is in his own world and seems happy to stay there. I don't know any kids here, except Cam. And she's leaving.

I look up at the sky, remembering all the things Cam told me about her planet. It sounds pretty darn great.

Her showing up is the most exciting thing that's ever happened to me. She actually knows me better than anybody, when I think about it. Life will be very dull when she goes. Then I'll really be alone.

I try to think just what it is that I have to stick around here for. I ask myself: When you're there waiting with Cam, and a spaceship actually comes for her, are you going to refuse to go on the biggest adventure of your whole life?

"They like dogs," I say out loud, quoting Cam to Josie. Josie turns and licks my salty cheek.

"What do you think, girl?" I ask.

She gives the funny singsongy growl she makes when we're having a conversation and she's answering one of my questions.

"You're right," I say. "Only a person with a small view of things would pass up an opportunity like that."

We get up and go inside. Josie heads for her corner in the living room, circles a few times, and lies down. I go to my room, close the door, and sprawl on the bed. I stare into the darkness for what seems like a long time. The longer I lie there, the more sure I am of my decision.

If a spaceship does land, I'm getting on it.

When I hear a car coming up the driveway, I get under the covers and curl up on my side, my face turned to the wall. I hear the door from the garage into the kitchen open and close. I listen to footsteps coming down the hall and stopping outside my room. The knob turns slowly, and a thin sliver of light shines on the wall. Though I'm facing away from the door, I close my eyes, feigning sleep, and remain absolutely still.

"Owen?"

I try to breathe evenly, like a sleeping person.

"Are you awake?"

I don't answer.

"This audit is a nightmare. I was holed up in a meeting with an IRS guy and couldn't get away. I should have called, I know. But we are right down to the wire on this thing."

Ooh, your big audit, I think. *Nothing's more important than that.*

"I couldn't leave," he says.

Yeah, I know.

There's silence for a while. Just when it's gone on long enough that I think he must have walked away without my hearing, he says in a barely audible whisper, "I'm sorry."

I almost turn around then, but I don't. What's the point?

The door closes, and I take a deep breath. I fall asleep and dream of a spaceship landing in a wheat field.

15

I WAKE UP EARLY, BEFORE DAD. QUICKLY, I FEED Josie and eat some cereal. Then I pack food for Cam and me, along with some water, dog food, and Milk-Bones. I leave a short note on the kitchen counter.

Got some stuff to do. See you later.

Owen.

It's vague, but offhand enough not to raise any suspicions. At least, that's what I hope. I want him to think it's just a day like any other.

I read it over and add the word "Love" before my name. I'm not sure why, but I don't feel mad anymore. I guess I feel kind of sorry for him. He's the one who's going to be left behind.

If the spaceship comes.

I'm about to leave when I think about packing some stuff to take with me. I hear the words in my head: *in case I never return.* I put my two favorite World Cup soccer T-shirts into my backpack, along with a pair of boxers. I take a look around my room to see what else I might miss. I hate to leave my posters, the model airplanes I worked so hard on, and my rock and fossil collections. But they're all too impractical to pack. Pinned to my bulletin board is a picture of me and Dad somebody took at an office Christmas party last year. It's a dumb picture, because the photographer made us put on Santa Claus hats, but I grab it anyway and shove it between the folds of the T-shirts.

Then Josie and I sneak out of the house. I see my soccer ball lying in the grass where I left it last night, and after a minute of indecision I put it in my backpack. Any decent planet has got to have soccer, right?

Josie and I hit the road. This is very possibly my last day on Earth, I think with a sharp thrill. It promises to be a beauty, too.

Mr. Powers's store appears to be open, even at this early hour, and I stop to buy a last bag of Tootsie Rolls for Cam. She said she wanted to take some back home with her.

I wonder again what the spaceship will look like.

When Josie and I walk into the store, Mr. Powers looks surprised. "What's got you and the hound out and about at this hour of the morning?" he asks.

I smile, wondering how high his fuzzy eyebrows would shoot up if I said, *Oh, we're taking off tonight for another planet, and we wanted to say goodbye.*

Instead, I say, "Oh, nothing much. Just an early morning bike ride." I grab a bag of Tootsie Rolls and put them on the counter.

Mr. Powers commands Josie to sit, says, "Good hound," and gives her a Slim Jim. He rolls me a jaw-breaker before taking my money. Then he eyes me with interest. Too much interest. "You two are up to something. Don't try to kid a kidder."

"What do you mean?" I ask, trying to look innocent.

He ignores my question. "Whatever it is, I hope it doesn't have anything to do with that big-neck fella. He's bad news, you can take that to the bank."

I don't say anything and Mr. Powers shakes his head. "Every day, I see you out running around loose," he says. "I ask myself, Where are that boy's parents?"

I wish I'd skipped the Tootsie Rolls, given Mr. Powers a farewell wave from the road, and kept on going. I'd be edging my way to the door now except he hasn't given me my change yet. "Oh, you know," I say. "Working."

"Hmmm," he says. He holds out his hand with my change in it, and adds, "Well, whatever you're up to, you be careful now, you and the hound. You hear?"

"I—we will," I say. This last comment of his seems nice, rather than nosy, and makes me feel more kindly toward him. I realize with surprise that I will miss my visits to old Mr. Powers's store. "And thanks for all the jawbreakers and the Slim Jims."

He says gruffly, "More where they came from. Come get 'em any time."

"Okay. Thanks." I start to walk out, then turn back and say, "Bye, Mr. Powers."

He gives me a long, penetrating look and then a nod. I leave, feeling his eyes following me.

On my bike again, I zoom down the rutted dirt path onto the trail, trying to shake off the feel of those knowing eyes.

Josie races beside me, and I think about the morning we discovered the torn, red-stained bits of a white T-shirt and followed the trail of the "bloody guy." It was six days ago, though it feels much longer. I pedal along, realizing how many trips Josie and I have made up and down this path, and how odd it is to know this is possibly the last time we'll do it.

Maybe that's why everything looks and smells and sounds sharper than normal to me. Josie's always excited when she's free to race around in the woods, so it's hard to tell if she recognizes that this is a special day.

Some painted turtles are out sunning themselves on the mossy, half-sunken logs in a pond, and their red-and-yellow throats look especially bright. They slip silently under the duckweed that floats on the pond's surface. I don't think I ever before noticed the incredible neon green of those weeds.

One by one, frogs hidden by the water's edge croak

and jump into the water with loud plops. This drives Josie wild. She races over to the edge of the pond, stares into the water, and then looks at me as if to say, *You heard that, too, right? So where did they go?*

A male wood duck takes off, making his squealing call. Then I see a hen with a string of ducklings swimming behind her. Her mate had flown off, trying to distract me from the babies. On the other side of the pond is a dead tree with a big hole in the trunk, where I bet she had her nest. I feel kind of sad to think I won't be here to see the ducklings grow.

I brush off these misgivings, reminding myself that Cam said there are dogs on her planet. If there are dogs, there have got to be other animals, too.

Soon I get to the place where I know Cam's tent sits right above me. I stop and look up, but I can't see any sign of it. There's nobody else on the trail this early, not even Ernie and Charlene, and I'm tempted to call out to Cam but decide not to take the chance.

I stash my bike extra carefully and start up the hill. "This could be the last time we have to climb this bugger," I tell Josie. "Not that it ever bothered *you*."

At the top, I walk along the edge, lean over where the tent sits below, and say in a cheery, singsong voice, "Rise and shine, *Cam*-per! Get it? *Camper*?"

After a few seconds I hear the sound of the tent door unzipping, and Cam crawls out. She blinks in the sudden brightness, yawns, and says grumpily, "Maybe it's

good you're not coming with me. I don't think my people are ready for your blazing wit."

I grin down at her. "Well, they're just going to have
to deal with my sophisticated ways. 'Cause if they show
up, I'm going with you."

She peers at me, her mouth falling open in a little O.
For once, I've managed to throw Cam off balance.

"You mean it?" she asks softly.

The hope in her voice makes my heart do a little flip.
I nod. "If that ship comes, I'm on it."

"You're sure?" Cam asks.

I nod again.

"What about your dad?" she asks.

"It might take him a couple days to notice I'm
gone," I say, "but then he'll be fine." I can feel her hesitation, and I give her another big grin.

She keeps looking at me. "Are you sure?" she says.
"I don't know . . ."

I laugh. "Cam! You've been bugging me to come
with you, and now you're going to try to talk me out of
it? Come on."

Suddenly she laughs, too, and her face turns to pure
happiness. "If you change your mind once we get there,
I'm sure they'll bring you back," she says.

"That's good to know," I say. "Now, would you
hurry and get up here? We need to talk about building
that signal."

16

I TAKE A BOX OF STRAWBERRY POP-TARTS FROM MY backpack, but keep the bag of Tootsie Rolls hidden to surprise Cam with later. As we eat, I ask Cam to explain to me exactly how we are going to build a signal using only a board, a hammer and nails, some rope, and a tape measure.

"A board, a hammer and nails, some rope, a tape measure, and a *stick*," she corrects me.

"Oh, a *stick*. That really clears things up."

Cam rolls her eyes. "Come on. We need to find a fairly sturdy stick about five feet long, nice and straight."

We look around until we find a dead branch that meets Cam's specifications. When I ask her again how we're going to make the signal, she says it will be easier just to show me. "And we can't begin until late this afternoon. If we're seen while we're doing this, it'll ruin everything," she warns.

We sit under the sycamore tree and pass the time teaching Josie to balance a Milk-Bone on her nose. She does it, but looks at us as if to say, *This is dumb. What's the point?* So we teach her to balance it, then flip it in the air and catch it. After a series of successful attempts, she loses interest, probably because she's bored.

When we eat lunch, I look at the huge open field. "That wheat only stands about three feet high," I say to Cam. "Anybody with eyes will see us when we're standing out there."

I don't mention Ray's name, but I'm sure she's thinking about him, too.

"I know. That's one reason we're waiting as long as we can. But I think the wheat's high enough to hide us if we crouch down. If someone comes, we should be okay if we hear them in time."

A small plane flies over, causing Cam to frown with concern. "That's our biggest worry. There must be a small airport over that way," she says, pointing. "I've noticed over the past few days they keep coming and going from there. They're flying low, too."

"If one of them spots us, what do you think they'll do?" I ask.

"It depends on how far along we've gotten with the signal, probably," she answers. "If they look down and see an obvious design, who knows? They might think it's interesting, and go on about their business. Or they might call their pilot buddies to have a look. Or they could call someone to report vandalism to a farmer's field. Or, they could call it in to the media." She makes a face. "That would be the worst."

I picture the drive to the deserted farmhouse swarming with TV vans and reporters. "That would not be good," I agree. "No spaceship will land if that happens."

"It's a chance we have to take," Cam says matter-of-factly. She gives me a happy smile and says, "But I refuse to believe that anything will go wrong. We're *so close*. We've got the ideal wheat field. We've got a full moon. You're my good luck charm, and you and Josie are coming with me. Everything's perfect."

Her confidence is contagious. I'm ready. I can't wait to get started.

Finally, when my watch says four-thirty, Cam says it's time. We walk toward the field carrying our materials. I'm wearing my backpack containing the food and drinks for us and Josie, my clothes, and my soccer ball.

We enter the wheat, Cam in front, me behind. "Try to have Josie follow right behind you," she tells me.

To Josie she says, "We can't have you racing around making your own designs, Josie. You'd probably spell out something like DOGS RULE THIS PLANET!"

"Knowing Josie, she'd more likely write DROP FOOD HERE!" I say. Then, in my command voice, I tell Josie to heel and, I swear, it's as if she senses this is important, because she does.

When we get to what appears to be the very center of the field, Cam stops, looks around, and, seeming satisfied, says, "Okay, we need to put the stick in the ground perfectly upright."

We try. But even though it rained the night before last, we can't get the stick to go into the ground deep enough to stand on its own.

I look at Cam, feeling anxious, wondering if this means the whole plan is doomed.

"I *knew* you were meant to be with me on this, Owen," she says. "Since there are two of us, we don't even need the dumb stick! You can stand here instead."

"Oh, great. I get it. *I* get to be the dumb stick."

Cam cracks up, then promises, "We'll take turns. After you watch me do one circle, you'll know what to do."

She takes the board and hammers a large nail into one end. Then she ties the rope firmly onto the nail.

"Can you hand me the tape measure?" she asks.

I do. She carefully measures off twenty feet of rope and says, "Hold the rope right here at the twenty-foot mark."

I say, "Yes, *sir*."

"Sorry. Didn't mean to sound bossy."

"Since when?" I ask, smiling to let her know I'm joking.

"Okay, now watch! I'm going to start the first circle."

"I just stand here and hold the rope at twenty feet, right?"

"Right."

Josie and I watch as Cam walks delicately through the wheat until the rope tightens. Then she puts the board on the ground, bends down, and starts pushing the board along. It takes me a few seconds to see what's happening. The wheat bends over and gets flattened as the board passes over it. By keeping the rope tight, Cam is making a four-foot-wide swath in the wheat, in a perfect circle twenty feet from the center point: me.

"Stay right there, but turn with me," Cam calls. "And keep your eyes peeled for anybody coming."

I do. It takes a pretty long time to make the full circle, and when Cam returns, she is red-faced and sweaty from bending over and pushing.

"It *is* simple," I tell her. "But it's also very cool. I wish I could see it from the air!"

"You will, when we take off." She hands me the board and smiles. "Your turn. Forty feet this time. I went clockwise, so you go counterclockwise."

"So the wheat will be mashed down in the opposite direction," I say. "That's important, huh?"

"It's a nice artistic touch. My parents will appreciate that."

So I start my circle forty feet from Cam, pushing in the opposite direction. I'm afraid Josie will come after me, messing up my pattern, so I tell her to stay, and she seems content to sit by Cam.

It's really hard work. When I get back to Cam I say, "No fair. My circle was twice as big as yours!"

"Yeah, but now I have to do sixty feet," she says.

She takes a big slug of water and then asks, "Did you see that plane?"

"What plane?" I ask with alarm.

"Another small one flew over, maybe about a quarter mile that way," she says, pointing south. "It just kept going, though, and didn't act suspicious."

"I never even heard it," I say. Which isn't surprising, really. The wheat stalks make a pretty loud crunchy noise as they're pushed over, plus I was facing down and concentrating on making my swath.

We measure off sixty feet, and Cam sets out into the wheat.

I'm standing there, holding my end of the rope and daydreaming about life on another planet. Cam told me her home is similar to Earth, but how similar? I have so many questions to ask her. I'll have time after we've finished the signal, when we're lying in the center of the circle, watching and waiting . . .

A sound snaps me out of my daydream. A car is coming up the gravel drive to the farmhouse, raising a cloud of dust behind it. I drop to my knees, grab for Josie's collar, and desperately follow the line of rope with my eyes. I see Cam—or her bent back and rear end, anyway. I'm sure she hasn't heard the car.

I jerk hard on the rope to get her attention.

"Hey!" she protests, standing up and looking in my direction. I point frantically toward the farmhouse. She doesn't waste any time looking, just drops down out of sight.

I lie down flat on my belly, one arm around Josie, another on her snout, ready to clamp down if she makes a sound. Luckily, she seems to think this is a neat new game we're playing and stays very still, her eyes locked on mine.

I strain to listen, and think I hear a car door slam, then another, and voices. Has Ray figured out where the old Davie place is? Or could it be the sheriff and a deputy, returning for another look around? The real estate lady and a customer? A furious farmer and his hotheaded, shoot-first-ask-questions-later hired man? A TV news van with a full crew? Did whoever it is see us? Is someone headed out into the field at this very moment, as Cam and I wait like sitting ducks? All the possibilities race through my mind until I can't stand it anymore and poke my head up for a quick peek.

To my surprise, there are three vehicles parked outside the farmhouse: a silver pickup, a little green car, and a black jeep. There are a bunch of high school kids fooling around, laughing and hollering and chasing each other as they unload coolers and blankets and towels. It looks like they're planning a party. I can't believe it. Are they really going to picnic in the yard of the farmhouse?

Music blares suddenly. One of the guys hoists a big CD player to his shoulder, and two of the girls start dancing around the yard. Nobody is looking out at the wheat field, so I keep my head up. I see the very top of

Cam's head peeking over the wheat stalks, and I know she is watching, too.

To my relief, the kids head to the edge of the hill overlooking the trail and, one by one, disappear. They're going to have their party down by the stream, maybe at the old mill site, not up here.

Whew.

There's no telling how long the party will last, though. At some point, those kids will be back to load up their cars and go home. The good news, I guess, is that a bunch of teenage partiers aren't likely to care what two younger kids like us are doing, even if they do happen to see us in the field. It'll probably be dark by then, anyway.

I stand up and give the rope another tug and after a couple seconds Cam, too, is standing. Then she pulls the rope taut and continues her slow, circular movement around me.

This circle takes a really long time. When Cam returns to the center, her hair is messed up and wild-looking, filled with dust and bits of wheat and plastered to her forehead with sweat.

I hand her the water bottle and she gulps noisily. "Close call," I say, "but it could have been worse."

She nods and takes a final swallow.

"My turn," I say.

"Have fun," she tells me, with a tired smile. "And go the other way."

"Right."

Bending down in a crouch, keeping my butt low, I scooch along with little baby steps, knocking down wheat stalks with the board, sweating. Not really what I'd call fun, especially since, from my ant's-eye view, the signal we're making doesn't look like much.

I do come across some interesting things, though, like a nest made from weedy stalks and leaves built in a little hollow on the ground. Inside are thirteen olive-greenish eggs. Judging from the size, I figure I scared off a momma pheasant. I move the nest over, out of the path of my board, and hope she'll find it when she returns.

Farther along, I see a few smaller, songbird-size nests, a woodchuck hole, and a green-and-yellow striped snake that glides in front of my board for a while before it wises up and escapes sideways. There are all kinds of bugs, too: grasshoppers leaping every which way, spiders, ants, and I don't know what other kinds of buzzing, crawling critters.

Suddenly I'm aware of a steady hum that isn't coming from any insect. I look up and, sure enough, there's another small plane flying almost directly overhead. I freeze until the hum fades. I'm about to start my circle again when the noise of the plane's engine begins to get louder, and I see it's making a second pass over the wheat field.

No! I think, wishing I could slap it away like a giant

bug. *Get lost!* But the plane makes a third pass before droning off across the lake.

The eighty-foot circle seems to take forever. Finally I return to the center and fall down on my back in a sweaty heap. Josie whines nervously, but once she realizes I'm okay, she licks my face until I start to laugh.

I look up and see that Cam seems troubled.

"The plane?" I ask.

"Yeah," she says glumly. "It definitely acted suspicious."

"I thought so, too."

Cam shrugs. "Well, there's nothing we can do about it now, so I'd better get going on the one-hundred-footer."

"How many circles are we making?" I ask, trying to remember the picture Cam had drawn.

"Six. Your next one will be the last, at one hundred twenty feet."

The sun is getting lower and I glance at my watch. I'm amazed to see that it is almost seven o'clock. No wonder I'm starving. "Did you eat anything?" I ask.

Cam nods. "Josie and I both did. Don't worry, we left some for you."

"Thanks a bunch," I say as she heads out into the wheat.

"And I didn't even see those Tootsie Rolls in your backpack," she calls over her shoulder.

At a couple minutes after nine, we're finally finished. I'm lying on my back on the ground once again, feeling totally trashed, when another plane flies over, makes a second pass, and leaves.

Cam and I look at each other, then look away. Neither of us wants to say what we're thinking, which is that all of our hard work will be for nothing if somebody comes to investigate the circles tonight.

"It'll be dark soon. How about I make a daring raid on the tent," I suggest, "and get the sleeping bags?"

She looks at me with her eyebrows raised.

"We might as well be comfortable while we're waiting," I explain.

"I wish we'd thought of it before," says Cam. "But you're right, it would be nice."

"I'll be super sneaky," I say. "And super fast."

After surveying the area, I run through the wheat, across the yard, and over the ledge to where the tent sits like an alien orange mushroom. I grab the sleeping bags and slide the tarp out from under the tent, fold everything up in a ball, and run back across the yard. Cam pops up quickly and waves me on.

We spread out the tarp and arrange the sleeping bags on top. Josie turns in her usual circles before making herself at home between Cam and me, and we settle in. Josie falls asleep, unaware that this could be her final evening on Earth.

17

CAM, JOSIE, AND I LIE IN THE DARKENED FIELD. I keep thinking, *This could be the last time I'll lie on the ground of Earth, this could be the last time I'll see the sun set from Earth.* These thoughts make my heart thump faster. At the same time, the idea of never seeing Earth again leaves an achy emptiness in my chest.

I concentrate on savoring each chewy, sticky mouthful of our last meal on Earth: Tootsie Rolls. In answer to my questions, Cam tells me that the animals and birds on her planet are just like ours, except that they're not endangered or threatened.

"And soon you'll see for yourself!" she says happily. "I'm so glad you're coming, Owen. I'm not sure I could have left without you."

This both pleases and embarrasses me, and maybe

Cam is embarrassed, too, because she turns away, and we don't say anything more for a long while. It feels okay, just being quiet.

Later, I nudge Cam. "Hey, are you awake?"

"Wide awake."

"Look. The moon!"

It's coming up over the wheat stalks, full and round. We lie quietly, watching it rise and slowly change color from orange to white.

You really can't spend that much time looking up into the sky without imagining that there are other planets and other worlds out there. You can't help feeling really, really small compared to it all, either. I guess billions of people have had the same feeling, but that just shows how true it is.

I don't say it, but I'd feel even smaller if I were lying out here alone. I've never had a girl for a friend before, but that's what Cam is.

"Well, we sure got the full moon we needed," I say after a bit. "Guess we should be on the lookout for the ship, huh?"

"They won't come until well after midnight, I'm sure," she says. "The less chance of people being up and about, the better."

"Makes sense." I look at my watch. It's only a couple minutes after eleven.

Josie lets out a sudden bark, and I grab her snout to silence her. There are far-off voices, and music. It's the teenage kids coming up from the trail. We hear them talking, laughing, and finally getting into their cars and driving away.

Cam and I try to pass the time by telling jokes and playing word games, but it's not easy to focus and, finally, we give up and just watch the sky.

Anxiously, I scan the moonlit darkness, trying to catch the first glimpse of the spaceship. I'm afraid to close my eyes for even a second, and they burn from staring upward with such concentration.

"Look!" I say, jiggling Cam's arm and pointing skyward. "There! What's that?"

After a couple seconds, Cam says, "A satellite."

A while later I get faked out by a shooting star, and then by a faraway airplane. I decide to keep my mouth shut until I'm sure I see a spaceship.

If the real thing appears, I think, *you'll know.*

The night stretches slowly on. Too slowly. I have a lot of time to think, and I begin to have second thoughts about what I'm doing.

I tell myself it's not that I have a small view of things. I believe there are other planets out there that support life, and that Cam came from one of them. For her to return home is a no-brainer. From what she's told me about her brief time here on Earth, she's got no reason to stay.

It's not the same for me.

Yeah, my relationship with Dad isn't so hot. But compared to Cam's problems here on Earth, ours don't seem so bad. I've been moping and blaming everything on Dad, but lying here in the darkness I wonder if that's fair. I ask myself what I've done to make things better, and the answer is . . . not much.

I think about the night when I came home late and Planet Dad and I broke out of our separate orbits and *almost* connected. I begin to wonder if I'm giving up too easily on something big. Something important. I wonder if, instead of heading toward something new, I'm just running away. I feel a little unsure now.

Then I tell myself, *You have a chance to go to another planet!* And I think, *Of course you're going.* I remind myself that Cam said her parents will bring me back if I want. That settles me down a little.

I check my watch. It's a quarter of one. The moon is directly overhead now. The next time I check, it's five after one. I try not to look for a long time. One-twenty-five.

Josie snores softly, and I envy her calm obliviousness. I feel Cam beside me, rigid with anticipation. I try to imagine what it's going to be like for her to see her parents again after all this time.

I'm happy for her. But at that moment I know I won't be going with her after all.

Her planet sounds beautiful, but I can't help thinking of all the things I would miss about Earth if I left. There are all the animals and birds, the snakes and turtles and frogs and fish, the things Mom taught me to see, and to love. I think about packing the first snowball of the year, riding my bike, running on the trail, and playing soccer. Even mowing the lawn and raking leaves can be kind of fun when you're in the right mood.

I think of the wood duck nest I saw this morning. Suddenly, I really want to be around to see those baby wood ducks grow up. They need people to care about them here on Earth.

I think of Dad. I said it would take a couple days for him to notice I was gone, but I know that's not true—I'm sure he's worried about me right now. I think of him here all alone, first losing Mom, and then me.

I peek over at Cam, lying next to me, staring intently into the heavens, waiting. I really, really hope her family gets here safely. And I hope she'll be so glad to see them that she won't mind if I stay behind.

I'm not going to tell her my decision until it's time for her to go. Not because I'm chicken, but because I hope that then she might be able to understand.

Sometime later, I wake with a start. Someone is whispering my name. Cam. Something warm and furry is pushing at my hand. Josie. For a few seconds I have no idea where we are.

Then I remember! We're waiting for the spaceship. I can't believe I fell asleep.

Cam sits up. "Listen," she says tensely.

Struggling to emerge from sleep, I sit, too, and strain to hear what she hears. After a moment, I do. Steady but stealthy, the crunching of wheat stalks and the swish of the stalks against fabric. Footsteps. Someone is walking toward us through the wheat.

Josie lets out three sharp barks, and I grab her nose to hush her. Cam and I stare at each other, too frightened to speak. The footsteps come closer and we sit frozen, listening. My body remains paralyzed while a thousand thoughts rush through my brain, none of them good.

A flashlight beam pans across the tips of the wheat stalks. A loud, angry voice calls out, "Damn it, girl, I know you're out there, so just stand up where I can see you."

Cam grabs on to my arm so tight I feel her fingernails through my shirt. "Ray," she says in a frightened whisper.

There is silence for a minute except for Ray's steps, coming closer. Ray is making no attempt at stealth or silence now, but moving fast.

"I know where you are, so don't think you can get away," he says.

"How can he know where we are?" I mutter desperately. "He *can't* know."

He can't know, and yet he is heading directly for us. I don't know what I'm going to do, but I sure don't plan on being huddled helplessly on the ground when Ray's flashlight beam finds us. I let go of Josie's nose, and she leaps to her feet, barking.

"Stay here," I say to Cam. Without waiting for a reply, I hunch over and scoot several yards to the left of our sleeping bags before standing. Josie dashes toward the flashlight beam, then races back to me, barking wildly. She is caught for a second, fully illuminated. Then the beam falls on me and zeroes in on my face. I squint against the brightness and shield my eyes with my hand.

"Where is she?" Ray says. He sounds almost bored as he says this, as if he knows I'm no match for him and he just wants to get it over with. As if I'm no more than the pesky bug he shooed away in the store. It makes me mad.

"You leave her alone," I say. My voice comes out high and shaky, and I stop to swallow. "Just leave her alone." I sound ridiculous, I know. This makes me even madder.

Ray chuckles, but it's not a jolly sound. "Sure, kid. I just need to talk to her first. Where is she?"

He has stopped walking, but continues to shine the light in my eyes. From behind its glare, he appears to me as a large, black, faceless form. He ignores Josie, who is circling him, barking like mad.

"Look," I say. "She's going away for good, somewhere far away."

He gives a snorting laugh.

"Just go and leave her alone." I hate the pleading note in my voice, but I can't help it.

"Kid. Shut up. Where is she?" Ray repeats. He sounds tired and his voice is impatient now, flat and mean.

I'm hoping that Cam is making an escape somehow, sneaking away while the flashlight is trained on me. If Cam runs off now, he won't be able to catch her.

I guess Ray is thinking the same thing because he turns the flashlight away from me and begins scanning the surrounding area. My eyes follow the light and—*no!* There's Cam, standing right where I left her. She's caught in the brutal beam, and turns her face away from it.

Ray reaches her in seconds. Before I know what's happening, he's dropped the flashlight and grabbed her. He's towering over her, holding her by both arms and shaking her.

"You little brat, if it was up to me, I'd have taken off and left you. You want to run away, it's *fine* with me. But your mother says I gotta find you, so she can kick your little smart-ass butt."

What is he talking about, "your mother"?

"Leave her alone!" I scream, running toward them.

Josie, hearing my cry and seeing Cam struggling with Ray, begins a frantic, high-pitched yelping. In the gleam from Ray's fallen flashlight I can see her jumping and hurling herself at their grappling bodies. I come from behind and grab Ray's arms. Cam dodges to the right, and Ray shakes me off and turns to face me.

"You little . . ." he mutters. He's so close I can smell his breath, and I realize he's been drinking. Then his fist comes flying at me. I turn away quickly enough so that it misses my face, but it catches the side of my head in a shimmering burst of pain. I fall to the ground from the force and surprise of the blow, and the dark, hulking shadow that is Ray looms over me.

Everything is happening in a dim, chaotic blur of noise and movement. Cam is screaming for Ray to stop, and Ray is panting, and Josie is growling and lunging like a wild thing. I've never seen her act this way, but we've never been in a situation like this before.

There's a dull thud, and a new wave of pain shoots through my side. I see Ray's boot moving backward to launch another kick, and I roll over, cover my head with my hands, and tense my body for the impact.

But it doesn't come. Instead, I hear a sudden crack, followed by a weird groan, and then I feel a heavy weight fall on top of me. It takes me a few seconds to realize it's Ray's body. This sends an almost electric surge of revulsion through me, and as I struggle frantically to get him off me, he lets out a soft moan and becomes still.

I crawl away from him and sit up, trying to figure out what's happening. When it's clear that Ray is not going to move, let alone launch another attack, I look up to see Cam standing a couple feet away.

The four-foot board we used to make the signal hangs from her hands. Her expression is hard to read in the faint light from the fallen flashlight, but she appears stunned.

Josie whines and licks my face, and I reach out a shaky hand to give her a pat. Cam remains frozen in place, staring at the board in her hands.

I say her name, but she doesn't answer.

"You—you hit him?" This seems amazing, and not quite real.

No answer. Then she whispers, "Is he . . . ?"

As if in answer to her unstated question, Ray stirs slightly and whimpers.

I see relief flood across Cam's face, and realize she was afraid she had killed him. The possibility of his death doesn't bother me in the least, not right at this moment, anyway. He had, after all, been trying his darnedest to kill me. But it appears he's only been knocked unconscious.

Slowly, I stand up. I feel a little dizzy. There's a wicked pain where Ray kicked me. But Ray is lying helpless on the ground and I'm alive. I can't quite believe what has happened.

Suddenly I become aware of a whooshing, whomping, droning noise coming from the sky. Cam and I both look up and listen. The sound grows louder.

And there it is, coming out of the eastern sky, directly toward us, with red lights flashing and white lights piercing the still-dark sky.

The spaceship!

18

THE NOISE GROWS LOUDER AND THE LIGHTS COME closer. A beam of light shines from the ship onto the field, moving methodically back and forth across the wheat.

Cam begins jumping up and down and waving. "Here we are!" she calls. "Here we are!"

In her excitement, she turns and hugs me. "Owen! They're here! They're really here!"

I'm shouting, "I know! I know! I can't believe it!" And I really can't believe it. But there is the ship! I look down at Ray, who isn't going anywhere anytime soon. But Cam is! The spaceship is here! It's zeroing right in on our signal!

As the ship draws nearer, I strain to make out its outline—is it a saucer shape, or more like a rocket, or a plane?—but I'm completely blinded by the beam of the searchlight. Although I can't see the ship, I can feel the powerful force of it, and the noise has become deafening. Cam's hair flies wildly about her face, and Josie barks with excitement, and I've never in my life had a feeling anything close to this, better than every single birthday and Christmas I've ever had put together.

The searchlight remains directly on us. We wave happily as the craft hovers above us, deciding, I imagine, where to land. Or maybe Cam will be beamed up into it! We wave and smile, waiting for instructions, or for the ship to make a landing.

Suddenly a deep voice blares out over the racket coming from the ship.

"Owen McGuire!"

I'm stunned for a second. How do they know my name? Why are they calling to me instead of Cam?

Cam and I gawk at each other, perplexed. Josie barks crazily at the strange deep voice coming from out of the sky.

Again, it booms through the night. "Owen McGuire. Return to the farmhouse with your companion. Repeat: return to the farmhouse immediately."

I can't believe this is happening. Cam and I simply stare at each other, too shocked to speak or move. With a rush of embarrassment and a disappointment so intense I feel kind of sick, I realize that the ship is nothing more than a helicopter. The wind and noise are coming from its whirling blades.

It rises a little higher and moves off to the west, but

continues to hover, the searchlight trapping us in its blinding cone of light.

More lights gleam from the direction of the farmhouse. I shield my eyes from the searchlight and make out car headlights and the whirling red roof lights of police cars in the driveway.

Cam stands staring into the sky. Her face is as still as a mask, except for the tears that roll silently down her cheeks.

I feel dazed and lost. From the terrible surprise of Ray in the wheat field to this—I have no idea what will come next.

And I know that however bad this is for me, it's much, much worse for Cam.

"Cam," I say. "What do you want to do?"

Cam doesn't respond, and I stand right in front of her and brush the hair away from her eyes, so she has to look at me.

Her lids flicker. Then, as if she's slowly pulling herself back from the edge of some dark place she's gone to in her mind, she looks up at me. The sun is just peeking over the tops of the wheat stalks and, in its fragile light, I see those amazing green eyes of hers. They are filled with so much sadness that I have to look away.

I quickly force myself to face her again. "Cam!" I say. "We don't have much choice, right? We have to go."

Cam, who has always acted so sure of herself, gives a shrug so slight I barely see it. She remains where she is, not able or not willing to move.

I've gotten used to turning to Cam for answers. She's the one who's been in charge. But it looks like it's my turn now.

I take her arm. "Come on. Let's go."

She doesn't resist, but she doesn't exactly help, either. She doesn't even react when Josie prances in front of us, wiggling and smiling and looking for attention.

After a few steps I say gently, "Cam? I'm sorry."

No answer. We take a few more slow steps.

"What happened? Do you know? I mean, did we have the wrong night . . . or the wrong kind of field . . . or the wrong signal?"

No answer.

"Cam, I'm trying to figure out what to do. I promised not to tell anybody about you, and I didn't. But look over there. The police are here. What are we going to tell them?"

Cam raises her eyes to mine. Her face crumples. She makes a horrible choking sound and starts to cry. She is sobbing, and she bends over and wraps her arms around her chest as if she's trying to keep herself from flying into pieces. I'm patting her on the shoulder and wishing there was some way I could help, but all I can do is just stay with her and wait.

The stupid helicopter is still hovering nearby, and I feel like shouting at it, *Get lost! Can't you see we're going?*

Finally Cam stops crying. Keeping her head down, she gasps out a few words mixed in with her cries and snuffles and hiccups. Her voice sounds broken. "When I was alone and scared—I imagined—I so wanted to believe—and then you came—and you made it seem possible—and you were even going to come with me— and now—I can't go back to Bobbi—Ray—I can't, I won't—"

And in a sudden rush of understanding, I get it: there is no Home Planet. There was never going to be a spaceship. This makes me sadder than anything I can re- member.

Cam raises her blotchy, tearstained face to mine and says, "I'm sorry, Owen. Some of it was true—Ray coming to live with us, moving to the motel, the way he treated me. Now there's nowhere for me to go. What am I going to do?"

Oh, man. I lie. I tell her not to worry. I tell her everything will be all right. I tell her there's a solution to all this, we just haven't thought of it yet. I keep bab- bling at her until we reach the edge of the field and step onto the lawn of the farmhouse.

By now the sun is up. There are a couple of small planes flying around and another helicopter hovering over us. In the driveway of the farmhouse is the scene Cam had earlier posed as our worst-case scenario: cars, including Ray's, television news vans with satellite dishes on the roofs, and sheriff's patrol cars with their lights flashing. I see that a policeman is just about to en- ter the field with a German shepherd, and I raise one hand in a feeble wave of surrender.

Josie runs up to the police dog wagging her tail, but he is all business, standing at attention, his ears pricked straight up, waiting for a command.

"Josie," I call wearily. "Come."

Josie comes to stand beside me, and reporters with microphones rush toward us, followed by their crews with giant cameras hoisted on their shoulders. They're all shouting questions.

"Are you Owen McGuire?"

"Who's the girl?"

"Did you make those circles?"

"Are they messages to aliens from space?"

Snickers follow this question.

"Or are you the aliens?"

More laughter.

I ignore them all and say to the policeman with the dog, "There's a man out there. He's unconscious."

He lifts his eyebrows and I say, "He attacked us. We were just protecting ourselves."

The policeman nods and starts walking out into the wheat field.

A reporter is standing close to us, looking and speaking at a camera. "We have live footage of the so-called crop circles that mysteriously appeared in a wheat field in the town of Benton, in the Finger Lakes region of central New York state, and of the two children who are believed to have made them. Stay tuned for this story as it unfolds."

I glance at Cam. Her face is streaked and swollen, but I'm glad to see it's lost that blank, empty look. When she turns to the reporters, I see in her green eyes the same mixture of fear and defiance I saw that first day when I discovered her in the upstairs bedroom of the farmhouse. I'm not sure, but it seems like a good sign.

A state police car pulls up then, and with a jolt, I see my father get out of the back. He gazes around anxiously, and when he sees me our eyes lock. He looks tired and bewildered—and relieved. We stare across the yard at each other.

The other rear door of the police car opens and a stooped, white-haired figure emerges with difficulty from the seat. It's Mr. Powers!

The sheriff tells the reporters to stand back and leave us alone. "Once we sort things out, there will be an official statement for the press," he announces. "When *we* know what's going on, you'll know."

Then the sheriff comes over to Cam and me, accompanied by my father.

"Hi, Dad," I say. I am so glad to see him, but I don't know how to tell him this. Instead, because it seems rude not to, I add, "Uh, this is Campion."

Cam says quietly, "My full name is Campion Cooper."

Campion *Cooper*? Startled, I realize I never knew Cam's last name. Cooper. My third-grade teacher's name was Miss Cooper, for crying out loud. It's such an ordinary Earthling name, it takes me aback for a couple seconds.

But then, I tell myself, it looks as if Cam is an Earthling, after all. Though I would never call her ordinary.

"Hello, Campion," Dad says. Then he gives me a hug. "Owen, I—" he says.

I want to hug him back, but Mr. Powers interrupts us, shuffling up and fixing me with a triumphant stare. "I *knew* you were up to something!" he says. "I said so, plain as day, when you were in the store, remember?"

His eyes penetrate mine, waiting for an answer. I nod.

He gives me a satisfied nod in return, and goes on. "So when I heard on the scanner that pilots reported some peculiar designs appearing in the field right back here, I thought to myself, *Uh-huh. It's that kid.* And then I heard there's a boy missing, and I called in and I told 'em, I know which way that boy went. I told 'em I knew you were up to something with the rope and the boards and all-what-have-you, and the trips back and forth, back and forth, all day long."

He turns to Cam suddenly, winks, and says slyly, "I suppose you're the one with the sweet tooth?"

Cam looks puzzled, and a little alarmed. I don't blame her: when Mr. Powers turns the full force of his gaze on you, he's someone to be reckoned with.

"The Tootsie Rolls," he says.

"Yeah, I guess that would be me," Cam replies.

"Got to be careful, they'll rot your teeth," says Mr. Powers. "I'm proud to say I still have all my own teeth."

He opens his mouth to prove this to Cam, the way he did for me the other day. I glance at Dad, who appears surprised by the way Mr. Powers has barged in and taken over the conversation.

Then the sheriff politely tells Mr. Powers to wait in another officer's car. "Someone will take your statement and drive you back to the store," he says.

Mr. Powers, clearly unhappy at being asked to leave the center of the action, gets in his final word. "You're not a bad kid," he says. "I told 'em that." To Dad he says, "You his father?"

Dad nods.

"I was you, I'd keep a closer eye on him," Mr. Powers advises.

Dad looks at me and nods again. It feels like a promise.

The sheriff leads me, Cam, Josie, and Dad over to his patrol car and tells us to get in, saying, "We can have some privacy here."

When we're settled in the car, with Cam and me in the back, Josie between us on the seat, and Dad and the sheriff in the front, the sheriff closes the windows and puts on the air-conditioning. Then he turns around and says, "Suppose you two tell me what in the Sam Hill is going on here?"

19

Three weeks later

I DON'T KNOW IF ANYONE IN OUTER SPACE SAW our signal, but it sure attracted a lot of attention here on Earth. Cam and I were right to be worried about the small planes that flew over while we were working on the circle. Somebody took pictures of us, and the story of the mysterious design in the wheat field was featured on the late-night TV news.

Cam and I don't know exactly what happened after that. But what we guess is that Ray and Bobbi were watching TV, and when the news report gave the approximate location of the wheat field, Ray began to suspect that one of the people in the aerial photos was Cam. When the footage showed the deserted farmhouse nearby, Ray put that together with what he'd heard on the police scanner and came after us.

I think back on how mean and mad he was that night, and how he smelled like he'd been drinking. Now

I imagine him driving around in the dark on those twisty, backcountry roads, trying to find the gravel driveway leading to the farmhouse. I picture his frustration and his anger at Cam growing with every wrong turn.

Meanwhile, my dad had reported me missing, and the police were searching for me. Cam and I were lucky, I guess, that the police showed up just a short time after Ray.

It seems hard to believe, but Bobbi is really Cam's mother. Ray's not her father, just one of Bobbi's boyfriends. Cam says there were a lot of boyfriends, but that Ray was the worst. He hated having a kid around. He hit her and locked her in the motel room, just the way she told me, and she ran away after that.

It's also hard to believe that Bobbi didn't even report that her child was missing, but she never did. Ray told her he'd find Cam himself. Not because either of them really wanted her back, but because they knew there'd be trouble if Cam told anybody what Ray had done to her.

When the story came out, Ray was charged with endangering the welfare of a child. Bobbi was charged with abandonment and neglect, and she signed papers giving up custody of Cam.

Which meant that Cam wouldn't have to live with Bobbi, or any of Bobbi's boyfriends, ever again. But it left the terrible question of what would happen to her. Bobbi had told the authorities that she had no idea where Cam's father was. Which meant Cam was truly alone.

Then something very cool happened. The local TV news reporters continued to follow Cam's story. Because Charlene and Ernie knew me and were interested, they watched closely. When they learned that Cam had no home, they contacted Social Services to say that she could live with them if she wanted to.

She's been with them for a week now, and it's working out great. Sidney latched onto Cam right away, and the two of them are always together, like Josie and me. Cam and I can hardly believe that she's living right down the road from me with Charlene, Ernie, nineteen dogs, and seventeen cats! When I asked her how it was going, she said her new life feels a lot like the one she imagined for herself on her home planet.

I think the story about her happy home with loving parents on a wonderful, faraway planet came to her when she was alone in the farmhouse and everything was so bad for her she couldn't see a way out. She made herself believe it because she needed to believe in *something*.

Then I came along. And when I believed her story, it made it even more real to her.

I guess you could say we got carried away.

But I still believe it could have been true. I'm still convinced there are other living beings out there somewhere, and that someday soon they'll make contact with us. I hope they make contact with *me*.

In the meantime, Dad and I have made a new start, too. For one thing, we're talking—about all sorts of stuff, including Mom. We unpacked the boxes from the old house and started building the deck off the kitchen. We play soccer in the yard every night after dinner, with Josie joining in, and sometimes Cam and Sidney, too. Next weekend, we're going on a camping trip to the Adirondack Mountains.

I think sometimes about the night Cam and I lay in the warm, cozy tent with Josie, safe from the storm, talking and eating Tootsie Rolls and never wanting to leave. Cam admitted then that life on Earth has its strong points. As usual, she was right.